"Where have you be

"Getting this for you." He
wrapped bundle. It warme

Aurélie's defenses droppe
disbelief. "You bought me a gift."

He frowned, which in no way diminished the potency
of his chiseled good looks. "No, I didn't."

"Yes, you did."

He rolled his eyes. "Don't get too excited. Trust me.
It's nothing."

With great care, she peeled back the tissue. When she
realized what he'd done, she couldn't seem to utter a
word. She blinked to make sure what she was seeing
was real—a hot dog. He'd gotten her a hot dog.

"It's a metaphor." He shrugged as though he were
right, as if this silly little gesture meant nothing at all,
when to Aurélie, it meant everything. "With mustard."

She didn't fully understand what happened next.
Maybe she wasn't thinking straight after getting the
call from the palace. Maybe the thought of going back
home had broken something inside her. Maybe she no
longer cared what happened to her at all.

Because even though she knew it was undoubtedly
the gravest mistake of her life, Her Royal Highness
Aurélie Marchand grabbed Dalton Drake by the lapels
and kissed him as though she wasn't already engaged
to another man.

DRAKE DIAMONDS:
Looking for love that shines as bright
as the gems in their window!

Dear Reader,

Welcome back to Fifth Avenue! *The Princess Problem* is the second book in my Drake Diamonds series for Harlequin Special Edition. I'm so excited about this story because it's my first princess book, and I've wanted to write a royal romance for a very long time—probably since I was ten years old.

Her Royal Highness Princess Aurélie Marchand arrives in New York looking for an escape. She wants a last chance at freedom, even if she knows it comes with an expiration date. When she offers Dalton Drake the chance to display a secret Marchand family heirloom at Drake Diamonds in exchange for a chance to live as a normal, everyday New Yorker for two weeks, a royal bargain is struck. But Aurélie and her French bulldog soon turn Dalton's carefully structured world upside down. The holiday ends up having much bigger consequences than either of them intended.

The heart of this story isn't just about romance, it's also about living life to the fullest. I hope it inspires you to do something unexpected and fun. If you enjoy *The Princess Problem*, be sure to check out the first book in this series, *His Ballerina Bride*.

As always, thank you for reading!

Best wishes,

Teri Wilson

The Princess Problem

Teri Wilson

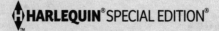

HARLEQUIN® SPECIAL EDITION®

Recycling programs
for this product may
not exist in your area.

ISBN-13: 978-0-373-62343-3

The Princess Problem

Copyright © 2017 by Teri Wilson

Printed in U.S.A.

Teri Wilson is a novelist for Harlequin. She is the author of *Unleashing Mr. Darcy*, now a Hallmark Channel Original Movie. Teri is also a contributing writer at HelloGiggles.com, a lifestyle and entertainment website founded by Zooey Deschanel that is now part of the *People* magazine, *TIME* magazine and *Entertainment Weekly* family. Teri loves books, travel, animals and dancing every day. Visit Teri at www.teriwilson.net or on Twitter, @teriwilsonauthr.

Books by Teri Wilson

Harlequin Special Edition

Drake Diamonds
His Ballerina Bride

HQN Books

Unmasking Juliet
Unleashing Mr. Darcy

Visit the Author Profile page
at Harlequin.com for more titles.

For my English writer friend
and fellow royal enthusiast, Rachel Brimble.

"The pearl is the queen of gems and the gem of queens."

Grace Kelly

Chapter One

It was the pearls that tipped Dalton off.

Dalton Drake knew a string of South Sea pearls when he saw one, even when those pearls were mostly hidden behind the crisp black collar of an Armani suit jacket. He stood in the doorway of his office, frowning at the back of the Armani-clad figure. The pearls in question were a luminous gold, just a shade or two darker than a glass of fizzy Veuve Clicquot. The rarest of the rare. Worth more than half the jewels in the glittering display cases of Drake Diamonds, the illustrious establishment where he currently stood. And owned. And ran, along with his brother, Artem Drake.

Dalton had grown up around pearls. They were in his blood, every bit as much as diamonds were. What he couldn't figure out was why such a priceless piece of jewelry was currently draped around the neck of a glorified errand boy. Or why that particular errand boy possessed such a tiny waist and lushly curved figure.

Dalton had paid a small fortune for a private plane to bring someone by the name of Monsieur Oliver Martel to New York all the way from the royal territory of Delamotte on the French Riviera. What the hell had gone wrong? It didn't take a genius to figure out he wasn't looking at a *monsieur*, the simple black men's suit notwithstanding. Delicate, perfectly manicured fingertips peeked from beneath the oversized sleeves. Wisps of fine blond hair escaped the fedora atop her head. She lowered herself into one of the chairs opposite his desk with a feline grace that wasn't just feminine, but regal. Far too regal for a simple employee, even an employee of a royal household.

There was an imposter in Dalton's office, and it most definitely wasn't the strand of pearls.

Dalton closed the door behind him and cleared his throat. Perhaps it was best to tread lightly until he figured out how a royal princess from a tiny principality on the French Riviera had ended up on Fifth Avenue in New York. "Monsieur Martel, I presume?"

"Non. Je suis désolé," the woman said in flawless French. Then she squared her shoulders, stood and slowly turned around. "But there's been a slight change of plans."

Dalton should have been prepared. He'd been researching the Marchand royal family's imperial jeweled eggs for months. Dalton was nothing if not meticulous. If pressed, he could draw each of the twelve imperial eggs from memory. He could also name every member of the Marchand family on sight, going back to the late 1800s, when the royal jeweler had crafted the very first gem-encrusted egg. Naturally, he'd seen enough photographs of the princess to know she was beautiful.

But when the woman in his office turned to face him, Dalton found himself in the very rare state of being caught off guard. In fact, he wasn't sure it would have been at all possible to prepare himself for the sight of Her Royal Highness Princess Aurélie Marchand in the flesh.

Photographs didn't do her beauty justice. Sure, those perfectly feminine features could be captured on film—the slightly upturned nose, the perfect bow-shaped lips, the impossibly large eyes, as green as the finest Colombian emerald. But no two-dimensional image could capture the fire in those eyes or the luminescence of her porcelain skin, as lovely as the strand of pearls around her elegant neck.

A fair bit lovelier, actually.

Dalton swallowed. Hard. He wasn't fond of surprises, and he was even less fond of the fleeting feeling that passed through him when she fixed her gaze with his. Awareness. Attraction. Those things had no place in his business life. Or the rest of his life, for that matter. Not anymore.

"A change of plans. I see that." He lifted a brow. "Your Highness."

Her eyes widened ever so slightly. "So you know who I am?"

"Indeed I do. Please have a seat, Princess Aurélie." Dalton waited for her to sit, then smoothed his tie and lowered himself into his chair. He had a feeling whatever was coming next might best be taken sitting down.

There was a large black trunk at the princess's feet, which he assumed contained precious cargo—the imperial eggs scheduled to go on display in the Drake

Diamonds showroom in a week's time. But there was
no legitimate reason why Aurélie Marchand had delivered them, especially after other transport had been so
painstakingly arranged.

Coupled with the fact that she was dressed in a man's
suit that was at least three sizes too big, Dalton sensed
trouble. A big, royal heap of it.

"Good. That makes things easier, I suppose." She sat
opposite him and removed her fedora, freeing a mass
of golden curls.

God, she's gorgeous.

Sitting down had definitely been a good call. A surge
of arousal shot through him, as fiery and bright as a blazing red ruby. Which made no sense at all. Yes, she was
beautiful. And yes, there was something undeniably en-
chanting about her. But she was dressed as a royal bodyguard. The only thing Dalton should be feeling right now
was alarmed. He sure as hell shouldn't be turned on.

Stick to business. This is about the eggs.

Dalton inhaled a fortifying breath. He couldn't recall
a time in his entire professional life when he'd had to
remind himself to stick to business. "Do explain, Your
Highness."

"Don't call me that. *Please.*" She smiled a dazzling
smile. "Call me Aurélie."

"As you wish." Against every instinct Dalton possessed, he nodded his agreement. "Aurélie."

"Thank you." There was a slight tremble in her voice
that made Dalton's chest hurt for some strange reason.

"Tell me, Aurélie, to what do I owe the pleasure of
a visit from a member of the royal family?" He tried
not to look at her crazy costume, but failed. Miserably.

"Yes, well…" There was that tremble in her voice

again. Nerves? Desperation? Surely not. What did a royal princess have to feel desperate about? "In accordance with the agreement between Drake Diamonds and the monarchy of Delamotte, I've delivered the collection of the Marchand imperial eggs. I understand your store will be displaying the eggs for fourteen days."

Dalton nodded. "That's correct."

"As I mentioned, there's been a slight change of plans. I'll be staying in New York for the duration of the exhibit." Her delicate features settled into a regal expression of practiced calmness.

Too calm for Dalton's taste. Something was wrong here. Actually, a lot of things were wrong. The clothes, the sudden appearance of actual royalty when he'd been dealing with palace bureaucracy for months, the notable absence of security personnel…

Was he really supposed to believe that a member of the Marchand royal family had flown halfway across the world with a trunkful of priceless family jewels without a single bodyguard in tow?

And then there was the matter of the princess's demeanor. She might be sitting across from him with a polite smile on her face, but Dalton could sense something bubbling beneath the surface. Some barely contained sense of anticipation. She had the wild-eyed look of a person ready to throw herself off the nearest cliff.

Why did he get the awful feeling that he'd be expected to catch her if something went wrong?

Whatever she was up to, he didn't want any part of it. For starters, he had more important things to worry about than babysitting a spoiled princess. Not to mention the fact that whatever was happening here was in strict violation of the agreement he'd made with the palace. And he wasn't about to risk losing the eggs. Press releases had been sent out. Invitations to the gala were in the mail. This was the biggest event the Drake Diamonds flagship store had hosted since it opened its doors on Fifth Avenue back in 1940.

"I see." He reached for the phone. "I'll just give the palace a call to confirm the new arrangements."

"I'd rather you didn't." Aurélie reached to stop him, placing a graceful hand on his wrist.

He narrowed his gaze at her. She was playing him. That much was obvious. What he didn't know was why.

He leaned back in his chair. "Aurélie, why don't you tell me exactly why you're here and then I'll decide whether or not to make that call?"

"It's simple. I want a holiday. Not as a princess, but as a normal person. I want to eat hot dogs on the street. I want to go for a walk in Central Park. I want to sit on a blanket in the grass and read a library book." Her voice grew soft, wistful, with just a hint of urgency. "I want to be a regular New Yorker for these few weeks, and I need your help doing so."

"You want to eat hot dogs," he said dryly. "With *my* help?" She couldn't be serious.

Apparently she was. Dead serious. "Exactly. That's not so strange, is it?"

Yes, actually. It was. "Aurélie…"

But he couldn't get a word in edgewise. She was going on about open-air buses and the subway and, to Dalton's utter confusion, giant soft pretzels. What was with her obsession with street food?

"Aurélie," he said again, cutting off a new monologue about pizza.

"Oh." She gave a little jump in her chair. "Yes?"

"This arrangement you're suggesting sounds a bit, ah, unorthodox." That was putting it mildly. He couldn't recall ever negotiating a business deal that involved soft pretzels.

She shrugged an elegant shoulder. "I've brought you the eggs. Every single one of them. All I ask is that you show me around a little. And let me stay without notifying the palace, or the press, obviously. That's all."

So she wanted a place to hide. And a tour guide. And his silence. *That's all.*

And face the wrath of the palace when they realized what he'd done? Have the eggs snatched away before the exhibit even opened? Absolutely not. "All the arrangements are in place. I'd have to be insane to agree to this. You realize that, don't you?"

"Not insane. Just a little adventurous." She was beginning to have that wild-eyed look again. He could see a whole secret, aching world in her emerald gaze. She leaned closer, wrapping Dalton in a heady floral aroma. Orchids, peonies, something else he couldn't quite place. Lilacs, maybe. "Live a little, Mr. Drake."

Live a little. God, she sounded like his brother. And his sister. And pretty much everyone else in his life. "That's not going to work on me, Your Highness."

She said nothing, just smiled and twirled a lock of platinum hair around one of her fingers.

Flirting wasn't going to work either.

He ignored the hair twirling as best he could and shot her a cool look. "The eggs are here, as agreed upon. Give me one legitimate reason why I shouldn't call the palace."

She was delusional or, at the very least, spoiled rotten. Did she really think he had time to drop everything he was doing to babysit an entitled princess? He had a company to run. A company in need of a fresh start.

He sat back in his chair, glanced at the Cartier strapped around his wrist, and waited.

He'd give her two more minutes.

That's all.

Aurélie was beginning to think she'd made a mistake. A big one.

Granted, she hadn't exactly thought this whole adventure through. Planning had never been her strong suit. Firing Oliver Martel and demanding that he hand over his suit so she could take his place on the flight to the States had been easy enough. That guy was an arrogant jerk. He needed to go, and he'd made enough passes at her over the course of his employment at the palace for her to have plenty of leverage over him. No problems there.

Impersonating a royal courier had also gone swimmingly. It was startling how little attention the pilot had paid her. He seemed to look right through Aurélie, as if she were a ghost rather than a living, breathing person. Then again, Aurélie had lived in a fishbowl her entire life. She was accustomed to being watched every waking moment of her existence. That's what this whole charade was about—getting away from prying eyes while she still could. In a few short weeks, her entire life would change. And, if her father got his way, she'd never get this kind of chance again.

Aurélie didn't regret walking away from her royal duties for a moment. Placing her trust in Dalton Drake, on the other hand, might not have been the wisest idea. For starters, she hadn't expected the CEO of Drake Diamonds to be so very handsome. Or young. Or handsome. Or stern. Or handsome.

It was unsettling, really. How was she supposed to make a solid case for herself when she was busy thinking about Dalton's chiseled jaw or his mysterious gray gaze? And his voice—deep, intense and unapologetically masculine. The man could probably read a software manual aloud and have every woman in Manhattan melting at his feet.

But it was his attitude that had really thrown Aurélie off-balance. She wasn't accustomed to people challenging her, with one notable exception. Her father.

That was to be expected, though. Her father ran a small country. Dalton Drake ran a jewelry store. She'd assumed he would be easy to persuade.

She'd thought wrong, apparently. But he would come around. He had to. Because she was *not* going to spend her last twenty-one days of freedom staring at the castle walls.

She swallowed. These wouldn't be her last twenty-one days of freedom. Her father would change his mind. But she shouldn't really be thinking about that right now, should she? Not while Dalton Drake was threatening to pick up the phone and tattle on her.

Give me one legitimate reason why I shouldn't call the palace.

Aurélie's heart beat wildly in her chest as she met Dalton's gaze. "Actually, Mr. Drake, I have a very good reason why you and I should reach an agreement."

He glanced at his watch again, and she wanted to scream. "Do elaborate, Your Highness."

"It's best if I show you."

She bent to open the buttery-soft Birkin bag at her

feet, removed a dark blue velvet box from inside and placed it square in the center of Dalton Drake's desk.

He grew very still. Even the air between them seemed to stop moving. Aurélie had managed to get his attention. *Finally.*

He stared at the box for a long moment, his gaze lingering on the embossed silver *M* on its top. He knew what that *M* stood for, and so did she. Marchand. "One of the eggs, I presume?" Clearly, Mr. Drake had done his homework.

"Yes." Aurélie offered him her sweetest princess smile. "And no."

Before he could protest, she reached for the box and removed its plush velvet lid. The entire top portion of the box detached from the base, so all that was left sitting atop the desk was a shimmering, decorated egg covered in pavé diamonds. Pale pink, blush enamel and tiny seed pearls rested on a bed of white satin.

Aurélie had seen the egg on many occasions, but it still took her breath away every time she looked at it. It glittered beneath the overhead lights, an unbroken expanse of dazzling radiance. Her precious, priceless secret.

She hadn't realized how very strange this would feel to share it with someone else. How vulnerable. She felt as though she'd unlocked a treasure chest and offered this strange man her heart. How absurd.

"I don't understand," he said, shaking his head. "I've never seen this egg before."

But there was a hint of a smile dancing on his lips, and when he trained his eyes on Aurélie, she could see the glittering egg reflected in the cool gray of his eyes, and she knew. She just knew.

Dalton Drake would agree to everything she'd asked.

"No one has," she said quietly.

She didn't know how she managed to sound so calm, so composed, when she was this close to having the one thing she'd wanted for such a long time. Freedom. However temporary.

He lifted a brow. "No one?"

"No one outside the Marchand family."

"So there's a thirteenth egg? I don't believe it," he said.

"Believe it, Mr. Drake. My father gave this egg to my mother on their wedding day. Other than the palace jeweler, no one even knew it existed." A familiar, bittersweet ache stirred inside Aurélie. She'd always loved the idea of her parents sharing such an intimate secret. Their wedding, their engagement and even their courtship had been watched by the entire world. But they'd managed to save something just for themselves.

What must it be like to be loved like that? To trust someone so implicitly? She'd never know, whether her father went through with his plans or not.

Of course, her parents' fairy-tale romance hadn't been as real as she'd always believed. Fairy tales never were.

Her throat grew tight. "I inherited it when my mother died three years ago. Even I was stunned to learn of a thirteenth egg."

Many things had surprised her then, but none so much as the shocking details of her parents' marriage. Her mother was gone, and Aurélie was left with nothing but the egg, a book with gilt-edged pages and a father she realized she'd never really known. And questions. So many questions.

When had things changed between her parents? Or

had the greatest royal romance of the past fifty years always been a lie?

Her eyelashes fluttered shut and memories moved behind her eyes—her mother and father waltzing in a sweeping circle beneath glittering chandeliers, the whirring of paparazzi cameras and her mother's elegant features setting into her trademark serene expression. A smile that never quite reached her eyes. How had Aurélie never noticed?

She opened her eyes and found Dalton watching her intently from across the desk. "Why are you showing this egg to me, Aurélie?"

Aurélie. Not Princess. Not Your Highness. Just her name, spoken in that deep, delicious voice of his.

Her head spun a little. *Concentrate.* "Because, I'd like you to display it in your exhibition."

"You're certain?"

"Absolutely." She paused. "On one condition."

Dalton gave her a sideways glance. "Just one?"

"Give me my adventure, Mr. Drake. On my terms. No bodyguards, no notifying the palace, no press. That's all I ask." And it was a lot to ask. She had enough dirt on the courier to guarantee he wouldn't go running to the palace. But someone would notice she'd gone missing. She just didn't know when.

It would be a miracle if she got away with this, but she had to try. She wouldn't be able to live with herself if she didn't.

She stood and extended her hand.

Aurélie had never in her life shaken a man's hand before. Certainly not the hand of a commoner. In Delamotte, Dalton wouldn't be permitted to touch her. Under royal protocol, he'd be required to bow from a chaste three-foot distance. "Do we have a deal?"

"I believe we do."

Then Dalton Drake rose to his feet and took Aurélie's hand in his warm, solid grip.

Delamotte had never felt so far away.

Chapter Two

"So let me get this straight." Artem Drake, Dalton's younger brother, pointed at the diamond-and-pearl-encrusted Marchand egg sitting in the middle of the small conference table in the corner of his office and lifted a brow. "You're saying no one has ever seen this egg before."

Dalton nodded and glanced over his shoulder to double-check that he'd closed the door behind him when he'd entered. He didn't want anyone else on the staff knowing about the egg. Its unveiling needed to be carefully planned, and he couldn't risk the possibility of a potential leak.

Satisfied with the privacy of their surroundings, Dalton turned to face his brother again and noted the enormous empty spot on the wall above his desk. The spot where the portrait of their father had hung for the better part of the past thirty years.

He was a bit taken aback by the painting's absence, since Artem hadn't mentioned his plan to remove it. And Drake Diamonds had never been about change. It was about tradition, from the store's coveted location on Fifth Avenue to the little blue boxes they were so famous for. Drake Diamond blue. The color was synonymous with class, style and all things Drake. It was the shade of the plush carpeting beneath Dalton's feet, as well as the hue of the silk tie around his neck. If Dalton were to slit his wrists, he'd probably bleed Drake Diamond blue.

But time changed things, even in places where tradition reigned. Their father was dead. This was no longer Geoffrey Drake's office. It was Artem's, despite the fact that there'd never been any love lost between Dalton's younger brother and their father. Despite the fact that Dalton himself had been groomed for this office since the day he'd graduated from Harvard Business School.

He was relieved the portrait was gone. Now he'd no longer be forced to stop himself from hurling his glass of scotch at it on nights when he found himself alone in the store after hours. Which was often. More often than not, to be precise.

Dalton averted his gaze from the empty wall and refocused his attention on Artem. There was no point in dwelling on the wrongness of the terms of their father's Last Will and Testament. He probably should have expected it. Geoffrey Drake hadn't been known for his sense of fairness. He certainly hadn't had a reputation as a loving family man. He'd been shrewd. Calculating. Brusque. As had all the Drake men, Dalton included, for as long as grooms had been slipping revered Drake Diamonds on their brides' fingers. Empires weren't built on kindness.

He leveled his gaze at Artem. "That's exactly what I'm saying. No one outside the Marchand family is aware of this egg's existence. Until now, of course."

Artem reached for the egg.

"Seriously?" Dalton sighed, pulled a pair of white cotton jeweler's gloves from his suit pocket and threw them at his brother. "Put these on if you insist on touching it."

Artem caught the gloves midair and shook his head. "Relax, would you? A secret Marchand imperial egg just fell into our laps. You should be doing backflips between the cases of engagement rings downstairs."

"We're on the tenth floor. Engagements is just down the hall, not downstairs," Dalton said dryly.

It was a cheap shot. Artem actually showed up to work on a regular basis now that they'd talked things through and agreed to share the position of Chief Executive Officer. The fact that Artem was now married and expecting a baby with their top jewelry designer, Ophelia Rose Drake, didn't hurt either.

Artem was a husband now, and soon he'd be a father. Dalton couldn't fathom it. Then again, he'd never actually witnessed a healthy marriage. To be honest, he wasn't sure such a thing existed.

Artem's features settled into the lazy playboy expression he'd been so famous for before he'd surprised everyone by settling down. "I know that, brother. You're missing the point. This is good. Hell, this is fantastic. You should be smiling for a change."

Dalton's frown hardened into place. "I'll smile when the unveiling of the collection goes off without a hitch. And when I'm certain I won't be facing jail time in Delamotte for kidnapping the princess."

"She came here of her own free will." With the hint

of a rueful smile, Artem shrugged. "Besides, the way I see it, you have a much bigger problem to worry about."

More problems. Marvelous. "Such as?"

"Such as the fact that you've been charged with showing a runaway princess a good time." Artem let out a chuckle. "Sorry, but surely even you can see the irony of the situation."

Dalton was all too aware he wasn't known as the fun brother. Artem typically had enough fun for both of them. In reality, his younger brother had probably had enough fun for the greater population of Manhattan. But that was before Ophelia. Artem's face might no longer be a permanent fixture on *Page Six*, but against all odds, Dalton had never seen him happier.

"Fun is overrated," Dalton deadpanned.

Fun didn't pay the mortgage on his Lenox Hill penthouse. It hadn't landed him on *Fortune*'s "40 Under 40" list for five consecutive years. And it sure as hell didn't keep hordes of shoppers flocking to Drake Diamonds every day, just to take something, anything, home in a little blue box.

Artem's smirk went into overdrive. "From what you've told me, the princess doesn't seem to share your opinion on the matter. It sounds as though Her Royal Highness is rather fond of fun."

Her Royal Highness.

There was a princess sitting in Dalton's office. And for some nonsensical reason, she was waiting for him to take her on a grand adventure involving hot dogs and public transportation. How such things fit into *anyone's* definition of a good time was beyond him.

A sharp pain took up residence in Dalton's temples. "Aurélie," he muttered.

Artem's eyebrow arched, and he stared at Dalton for a moment that stretched far too long. "Pardon?"

Dalton cleared his throat. "She's asked me to call her Aurélie."

"Really?" Artem's trademark amused expression made yet another appearance. To say it was beginning to grate on Dalton's nerves would have been a massive understatement. "This princess sounds rather interesting."

"That's one way of putting it, although I'd probably use another word."

"Like?"

Unexpected. "Impulsive." *Whimsical.* "Volatile." *Breathtaking.* "Dangerous."

"That's three words," Artem corrected. "Interesting. The princess—excuse me, *Aurélie*—must have made quite an impression in the twenty minutes you spent with her."

Twenty minutes? Impossible. It had been precisely 10 a.m. when he'd first set eyes on those golden South Sea pearls. On that straight, regal back and exquisitely elegant neck. If the severity of the tension between his shoulder blades was any indication, he'd been dealing with the stress of harboring a royal runaway for at least two hours. Possibly three.

Dalton glanced at his Cartier. It read *10:21*. He'd need to add a massage therapist to the payroll at this rate. *If* he managed to keep an aneurysm at bay for the next few weeks.

"I dare say you appear rather intrigued by her." Artem's gaze narrowed. "If I didn't know you better, I'd go so far as to say you seem smitten. But of course the Dalton I know would never mix business and pleasure."

Damn straight. Dalton preferred pleasure of the no-strings variety, and he seldom had trouble finding it. Sex belonged in the bedroom, not the boardroom. He wasn't Artem, for crying out loud. He could keep his libido in check when the situation called for it. "I assure you I'm not smitten. I have no feelings toward the princess whatsoever, aside from obligation."

"Ah yes, your bargain." Artem turned the egg in his grasp, inspecting it. Blinding light reflected off its pavé diamonds in every direction, making the egg look far more precious than a collection of carefully arranged gemstones. Dynamic. Alive. A brilliant, beating heart.

Dalton had never seen anything quite like it. The other Marchand imperial eggs paled in comparison. When it went on display in the showroom, Drake Diamonds would be packed wall-to-wall with people. People who wouldn't go home without a Drake-blue bag dangling from their arms.

If the egg went on display.

It would. The exhibition and gala would take place as scheduled. The spectacular secret egg was just what Drake Diamonds needed. When Dalton and Artem's father died, he'd left the family business on the verge of bankruptcy. They'd managed to climb their way back to solvency, but Drake Diamonds still wasn't anywhere near where it had been in its glory days.

Dalton aimed to fix that. With the egg, he could.

He would personally see to it that the palace in Delamotte had nothing to worry about. He'd keep Aurélie under lock and key. Then, in three weeks' time, she'd pack up the eggs and go straight home. Dalton would strap her into her airplane seat himself if he had to.

Artem returned the egg to its shiny satin pedestal, peeled off the jeweler's gloves and tossed them on the table. Then he crossed his arms and shot Dalton a wary glance. "Tell me, what sort of fun is the princess up to at the moment?"

Dalton shrugged. "She's in my office."

"Your office? Of course. Loads of fun, that place." Artem shot him an exaggerated eye roll.

This was going to stop. Dalton might have agreed to escort the princess on her grand adventure, but under no circumstances would he succumb to constant commentary on his personal life. "I've asked Mrs. Barnes to get her settled with a glass of champagne and a plate of the petit fours we serve in Engagements."

"So you have absolutely no interest in the woman, yet she's in your office snacking on bridal food."

Before Dalton could comment, there was a soft knock on the door.

The brothers exchanged a loaded glance, and Dalton swiftly covered the jeweled egg with the lid to its tasteful indigo box.

Once the treasure was safely ensconced in velvet, Artem said, "Come in."

The door opened, revealing Dalton's secretary balancing a plate of petit fours in one hand and a glass of champagne in the other, wearing a distinct look of alarm. "I'm sorry to interrupt…"

Dalton's gut churned. Something wasn't right. *But what could have gone wrong in the span of a few minutes?* "Yes, Mrs. Barnes?"

"Your guest is gone, Mr. Drake."

Surely she was mistaken. Aurélie wouldn't just take off and leave the eggs behind. She wouldn't think about walking around a strange city all alone, without her security detail.

Or would she?

Dalton swore under his breath. Why did he get the feeling that Aurélie would do both of those things without bothering to consider the possible disastrous consequences of her actions?

Live a little, Mr. Drake.

"Shall I take a look in the ladies' room?" Mrs. Barnes asked.

Dalton shook his head. If he thought for one second that Aurélie Marchand could be found in the ladies' room of Drake Diamonds, he'd march in there and go get her himself. "No, thank you. I'll see to her whereabouts. That will be all, Mrs. Barnes."

"Yes, sir." She nodded and disappeared in the direction of Dalton's office.

"Calm down, brother. I'm sure she hasn't gone far. She's not going to just disappear and leave the Marchand family jewels behind." Artem waved a casual hand at the velvet box in the center of the table.

Dalton sighed. "Have you forgotten that she's in a strange city? In a foreign country. All alone."

"Exactly. She's hasn't ventured any further than the Plaza. Come on, I'll help you track her down." Artem reached for the suit jacket on the back of his chair.

"No," Dalton said through gritted teeth. He pointed at the velvet box. "You stay, and see to it that the eggs are safely locked away in the vault. I'll find Miss Marchand."

And when he did, he'd lay down some ground rules for their arrangement. *After* he'd made it clear that he considered her behavior wholly unacceptable. Princess or not.

"As you wish," Artem said. "But can I give you one piece of advice?"

Dalton glared at him. "Do I have a choice?"

"Whatever you do, don't take her to bed." Artem's mouth curved into a knowing grin. "Assuming you find her, of course."

Who did Dalton Drake think he was?

She hadn't traveled halfway across the world, and risked the wrath of her father, only to stay trapped in a closed room on the tenth floor of Drake Diamonds. Not that the surroundings weren't opulent. On the contrary, the place was steeped in elegant luxury, from the pale blue plush carpet to the tasteful crown molding. It felt more like being in a palace than a jewelry store.

Which was precisely the problem.

She didn't want to be stuck inside this grand institution. It wasn't what she'd signed on for. Did he not realize the risks she'd taken to get here? She already had three missed call notifications on her cell from Delamotte. None from her father, thank goodness. It would take him days, if not weeks, to realize she was gone. The Reigning Prince had more important things to worry about than something as trivial as his only daughter fleeing the country. Oh, the irony.

But the palace staff was another story. They watched her every move and minced no words when it came to their opinions on her behavior. Or her fashion sense. Or her hair.

Or her love life. They had plenty to say about that.

How on earth was she going to pull this off? What if her father came looking for her?

She sighed. She wasn't going to think about that now. Besides, she was lost in the maze of pale blue and the sparkle of the diamond store. How would she find her way around New York when she couldn't even manage to navigate the terrain of Drake Diamonds?

Every room looked the same. Row upon row of diamonds sparkled beneath gleaming glass. Chandelier earrings. Long platinum chains with dazzling pendants shaped like antique keys. Shiny silver bracelets with heart-shaped charms.

Engagement rings.

Aurélie looked around and realized she was surrounded by couples embracing, holding hands and clinking champagne flutes together while they gazed into one another's eyes. Everywhere she turned, teary-eyed brides-to-be were slipping diamond solitaires on their fingers.

She felt oddly hollow all of a sudden. Numb. Empty. Alone.

For some silly reason she remembered the feel of Dalton's palm sliding against her own when they'd shaken on their deal. He had strong hands. The hands of a man accustomed to getting what he wanted. What he wanted right now was her secret egg, of course. She'd given it to him on a silver platter.

And now he was gone.

Her cell phone vibrated in her pocket. Again. Aurélie switched it off and removed the SIM card without bothering to look at the display. Without a SIM card, the GPS tracking on her iPhone wouldn't work. At least she thought she remembered reading that somewhere.

She really should have had a better escape plan. Or at least *a plan*.

Her gaze snagged on a silver sign hanging on the wall with discreet black lettering. *Will you? Welcome to the Drake Diamond Engagement Collection.*

She rolled her eyes, marched straight to the elevator and jabbed at the down button with far too much force.

But as she waited, something made her turn and look again, some perverse urge to torture herself. Maybe she needed a reminder of why she'd fled Delamotte. Maybe she wanted to test herself to see if she could stand there in the midst of so much romantic bliss without breaking down. Maybe she'd simply left the vestiges of dignity back in her home country.

She stared at the happy couples, unabashed in their affection, and felt as though she were disappearing. Fading into the tasteful cream-colored wallpaper.

None of this is real, she told herself. She didn't believe any of it for a minute.

She wanted to, though. Oh how she wanted to. She wanted to believe that happy endings were real, that love could last, that marriage was something more than just another transaction. A business deal.

A bargain.

But she didn't dare, because believing the fairy tale would hurt too much. Believing would mean admitting she was missing out on something she'd never have. Something worth more than deep crimson rubies, cabochon emeralds and the entire collection of imperial Marchand eggs.

Why was the elevator taking so long? She pushed the button a few more times, yet still jumped in surprise when the chime signaled the elevator's arrival. The doors swished open, and she half ran, half stumbled inside.

A hand caught her elbow. "Are you all right, miss?"

She blinked up at the elevator attendant dressed in a stylish black suit, pristine white shirt and a bowtie the same hue as the Windsor knot that had sat at the base of

Dalton Drake's muscular neck. Aurélie's gaze lingered on that soft shade of blue as she remembered how perfectly Dalton's silk tie had set off his strong jawline.

"I'm fine, thank you." The elevator closed and began its downward descent, away from all those engagement rings and the quiet solitude of Dalton's office.

The elevator attendant smiled. "Do you need help finding anything?"

Aurélie shook her head, despite the fact that she didn't know the first thing about New York. She didn't know how to hail a cab or ride the subway. She didn't even have a single American dollar in her fancy handbag. She had a wallet full of euros, yet she wasn't even familiar with the exchange rate.

But none of that mattered. She just wanted to get out of there.

Now.

Chapter Three

Right around the time he was on the verge of losing his mind, Dalton spotted Aurélie on the outskirts of Central Park. She was standing beneath a portable blue awning at the corner of Central Park South and 59th Street, directly across the street from the Plaza Hotel. She was holding a dog. Not a hot dog, but an actual dog. Which for some reason only exacerbated the pounding in Dalton's temples. The woman was impossible.

What had she been thinking? She didn't want to be discovered, yet she'd walked right out the door. Unaccompanied. Unprotected. Undisguised. It was enough to give Dalton a coronary.

At least he'd been able to find her with relative ease. All told, it had only taken about a quarter of an hour. Still, those fifteen minutes had undoubtedly been the longest of Dalton's life.

To top things off, a street musician had parked himself right outside the entrance of Drake Diamonds with his violin and his tip bucket. This marked the third time in less than a month that Dalton had ordered him to leave. Next time, he'd call the cops.

He squinted against the winter wind and shoved his bare hands into his trouser pockets. He'd been in a panic when he'd spun his way out of the store through the revolving door and onto the snowy sidewalk. Filled with dread and angry beyond all comprehension, he hadn't even bothered to grab a coat, and now, three blocks later, he was freezing.

Freezing and absolutely furious.

He dashed across the street without bothering to wait for the signal at the pedestrian crossing, enraging a few cab drivers in the process. Dalton didn't give a damn. He wasn't about to let her out of his sight until he'd returned her safely to his office. And then...

What?

He wasn't actually sure what he'd do at that point. He'd cross that bridge when he came to it. Right now he simply planned on escorting her back to his store on the corner of Fifth Avenue and 57th Street while administering a searing lecture on the dangers of disappearing without giving him any sort of notice whatsoever.

"Aurélie!" He jogged the distance from the curb to where she stood, still holding onto the damn dog.

She didn't hear him. Either that, or she was intentionally ignoring him. It was a toss-up, although Dalton would have greatly preferred the former.

"Aurélie," he said again, through gritted teeth, when he reached her side.

An older woman wearing a hooded parka and fin-

gerless mittens stood next to her. There was a clipboard
in her hands and a small playpen filled with little dogs
yipping and pouncing on one another at her feet. The
woman eyed Dalton, giving him a thorough once-over,
and frowned.

"Oh good, you're here," Aurélie said blithely, without tearing her gaze from the trembling, bug-eyed dog
in her arms.

It stared at Dalton over her shoulder. He stared back
and decided it was possibly the ugliest dog he'd ever set
eyes on. Its pointed ears were comically huge, which
might have been endearing if not for the googly eyes
that appeared to be looking in two completely different
directions. And it had a wide, flat muzzle. Not to mention the god-awful snuffling sounds coming from the
dog's smashed little face.

"Hello." The woman with the clipboard nodded. "Are
you the boyfriend?"

Boyfriend?

Hardly.

He opened his mouth to say no—*God no*—but before he could utter a syllable, Aurélie nodded. "Yes, here
he is. Finally."

Dalton didn't know what kind of game she was playing, and frankly, he didn't care. If she wanted to pose
as some kind of couple in front of this random stranger
who could possibly recognize her from the tabloids, then
fine. Although, the idea was laughable at best.

"Yes, here I am." He turned sharp eyes on her with
the vague realization that he wasn't laughing. Not even
close. "*Finally.* Surely you're aware I've been looking
for you, sweetheart."

At last she met his gaze. With snowflakes in her eyelashes and rosy, wind-kissed cheeks, she looked more Snow Queen than princess.

And lovelier than ever.

Nature suited her. Or maybe it was winter itself, the way the bare trees and dove-gray sky seemed to echo the lonely look in her eyes. Seeing her like this, amidst the quiet grace of a snowfall, holding onto that ugly dog like a child hugging a teddy bear, Dalton got a startling glimpse of her truth.

She was running from something. That's why she'd left Delamotte. That's why she'd shown up in men's clothes and begged him not to call the palace. She wasn't here on holiday. She was here to get lost in the crowd.

Not that her reasons had anything to do with Dalton. He was simply her means to an end, and vice versa.

"What's our address again? Silly me, I keep forgetting." She let out a laugh.

Dalton fought to keep his expression neutral. Surely she wasn't planning on moving into his apartment. That's what hotels were for. And there were approximately 250 of them in New York.

Then again, who knew what sort of trouble she could get into unsupervised.

His headache throbbed with renewed intensity. "*Our* address?"

"Of course, darling. You know, the place where we live." Quicker than a blink, her gaze flitted to the woman with the clipboard. "Together."

Struggling to absorb the word *darling*, he muttered the address of his building in the Upper East Side. The woman with the clipboard jotted it down.

Who was this person, anyway? And why did Aurélie

think she had any business knowing where they lived? *Where* I *live. Not* we. *Good God, not we.*

He leaned closer to get a look at whatever form she appeared to be filling out. The bold letters at the top of the page spelled out *Pet Adoption Agreement.*

"Wait," Dalton said, as something wet and foul-smelling slapped against the side of his face. He recoiled and realized, with no small degree of horror, that it was the googly-eyed puppy's tongue.

Marvelous. He wiped his cheek with the cuff of his suit jacket, and aimed his fiercest death glare at Aurélie. "What do you think you're doing?"

"*We* are adopting a dog, darling." Again with the *darling.*

And again with the *we.*

"I believe this is the type of thing we should discuss," he said, trying not to imagine the dreadful dog snoring like a freight train in his office while he tried to run the company.

Or, God forbid, snoring in his bed. Because if adopting homeless animals was the sort of thing she did on a whim when he wasn't looking, she'd need to stay with him. Who knew what kind of trouble she could get into if he left her all alone in a hotel room for a fortnight?

He'd been wrong when he'd described her to Artem as impulsive. *Impulsive* didn't even begin to describe Aurélie. She was full-blown crazy. Either that or the most manipulative woman he'd ever met.

"But we *did* discuss it. This morning." Her bow-shaped lips curved into a beguiling smile that hit Dalton square in his libido, despite the deafening clang of warning bells going off in his head.

She was business. She was irritating to no end. And

what's more, she was far too headstrong for his taste. He shouldn't be attracted to her in any way, shape or form. Nor should he be thinking about that troublesome mouth of hers and the myriad ways in which he'd prefer to see her use it.

She rested a hand on his bicep and gave it a firm squeeze. "Surely you remember our agreement?"

Unbelievable. She was using the secret egg to blackmail him into adopting a dog. She wasn't crazy at all. *Cunning.* Most definitely.

Dalton Drake didn't take orders. Nor did he allow himself to be manipulated in such a manner. Aurélie would learn as much soon enough. But not until he'd taken the pathetic animal home, apparently.

"Well?" The clipboard-wielding woman tilted her head. "What's it going to be? Do you want to adopt him or not?"

Aurélie nodded furiously. "Absolutely. We do. Right, darling?" She looked at him expectantly. So confident. So certain he'd acquiesce to whatever she demanded.

He had a mind to refuse and put her on the next plane back to the French Riviera, along with the dog and all of the Marchand family jewels. Yes, they had a deal. But it didn't encompass sending him on a wild goose chase. Nor did it include sharing his apartment. With her, or the dog.

He hadn't taken a woman into his home since Clarissa. But that had been a long time ago. He'd been a different man.

Think of the egg. What it could do for business.

He looked at Aurélie for a long moment, and for some ridiculous reason, Artem's warning came flooding back.

Whatever you do, don't take her to bed.

He wouldn't. Of course he wouldn't. The very fact that Artem had seen fit to mention the possibility was preposterous. Dalton wasn't the one who'd bedded half the women in Manhattan. That had been Artem's doing. Dalton's self-control was legendary.

But looking into Aurélie's aching emerald eyes did something to him. That vulnerability that she hid so well was barely noticeable, but very much there. And it made him wonder what she'd look like bare in the moonlight, dressed in nothing but pearls.

Damn you, Artem.

Then, before he could stop himself, he heard himself say, "Fine. We'll take the dog."

What kind of person didn't like animals?

The kind who was seething quietly beside Aurélie, evidently.

Dalton hadn't uttered a word since he'd paid the adoption fee and slipped the receipt into his suit pocket. He'd simply aimed a swift, emotionless glance at Aurélie, cupped her elbow in the palm of his hand and steered her back in the direction of Drake Diamonds. Now, less than a block later, he was walking so fast that she struggled to keep up with him. She had a mind to give up entirely and pop into the Plaza for afternoon tea, but looking at the tense set of Dalton's muscular shoulders as he marched in front of her, she got the distinct feeling there'd be hell to pay if she didn't fall in step behind him.

Plus she didn't have any money. Or credit cards. Which meant she was totally dependent on the very cranky Dalton Drake.

Besides, every three or four paces, he glanced over his shoulder, probably to assure himself of her obedience. It was infuriating, particularly when Aurélie recalled the archaic Delamotte law that stated royal wives must walk a minimum of two paces behind their husbands in public. No doubt a man had come up with such a ludicrous decree.

She held the trembling little dog tight against her chest and hastened her steps. She wasn't Dalton's lowly subordinate, and she refused to act like it. Even if, as they said in Delamotte, *la moutarde lui monte au nez*. The mustard was getting to his nose. In other words, he was angry.

Fine. So was she. And she wasn't spending another second scurrying to keep up with him.

"*Arrête!* Stop it." She tugged on his sleeve, sending him lurching backward.

Dalton's conservative businessman shoes slid on the snowy pavement, but he righted himself before he fell down. Pity.

He exhaled a mighty sigh, raked his disheveled hair back into place and stared down at her with thunder in his gaze. "What is it, Aurélie?"

She blinked up at him, wishing for what felt like the thousandth time, that he wasn't so handsome. His intensity would be far easier to take if it didn't come in such a beautiful package.

His gray eyes flashed, and a shiver coursed through Aurélie. As much as she would have liked to blame it on the cold, she knew the trembling in her bones had nothing to do with the weather. He got to her. Especially when he looked at her like he could see every troublesome thought tumbling in her head. "What do you want?"

What did she want?

Not this. Not the carefully controlled existence she'd lived with for so long. Not the future awaiting her on the distant shores of home.

She wasn't sure exactly what she wanted, only that she needed it as surely as she needed to breathe. She couldn't name it—this dark, aching thing inside her that had become impossible to ignore once her father had sat her down and laid out his plans for her future.

Palace life had never come easily to Aurélie. Even as a child, she'd played too hard, laughed too loudly, run too fast. Then that little girl had grown into a woman who felt things too keenly. Wanted things too much. The wrong things.

Just like her mother.

Aurélie had learned to conduct herself like royalty, though. Eventually. It had been years since she'd torn through the palace halls, since she'd danced with abandon. She'd become the model princess. Proper. Polite. Demure.

But since the awful meeting with the Reigning Prince and his advisors a month ago, her carefully constructed façade had begun to crack. She couldn't keep pretending, no matter how hard she tried.

What do I want? She couldn't say, but she'd know it when she found it.

Dalton glowered at Aurélie.

She inhaled a breath of frigid air and felt as if she might freeze from the inside out. "Are you always this cranky?"

He arched a single, accusatory brow. "Are you always this irresponsible?"

"Irresponsible?" The nerve. He didn't know a thing

about her life in Delamotte. "Did I just hear you correctly?"

People jostled past them on the sidewalk. Skyscrapers towered on either side of the street. The snow was coming down harder now, like they were inside a snow globe that had been given a good, hard shake.

"You certainly did," he said.

God, he was rude. Particularly for a man who wanted something from her. "You do realize who you're speaking to, don't you, Mr. Drake?"

He looked pointedly at the puppy in Aurélie's arms.

The little dog whimpered, and she gave him a comforting squeeze.

If she put herself in Dalton's shoes, she could understand how adopting a dog on a whim might appear a tad irresponsible. But it wasn't a whim. Not exactly. And anyway, she shouldn't have to explain herself. They had a deal.

He crossed his arms. Aurélie tried not to think about the biceps that appeared to be straining the fabric of his suit jacket. How did a man who so obviously spent most of his time at work get muscles like that? It was hardly fair. "You said you wanted a hot dog, not a French bulldog."

What was he even talking about? Oh, that's right— her grand speech. "The hot dog was a metaphor, Mr. Drake."

"And what about the pretzel? Was that a metaphor, as well?"

"No. I mean, yes. I mean…" *Merde.* Why did she get so flustered every time she tried to talk to him? "What do you have against dogs, anyway?"

"Nothing." He frowned. How anyone could frown in

the presence of a puppy was a mystery Aurélie couldn't begin to fathom. "I do, however, have a problem with your little disappearing act."

"And I have a problem with your patronizing attitude."

She needed to put an end to this ridiculous standoff and get them both inside, preferably somewhere other than Dalton's boring office. "I could very easily pack up my egg and go home, if you like."

"Fine." He shrugged, and to her utter astonishment, he began walking away.

"I beg your pardon?" she sputtered.

He turned back around. "Fine. Go back to your castle. And take the mutt with you."

A slap to the face wouldn't have been more painful. She squared her shoulders and did her best to ignore the panicked beating of her heart. "He has a name."

"Since when? Five minutes ago?"

"It's Jacques." She ran a hand over the dog's smooth little head. "In case you were wondering."

A hint of a smile passed through his gaze. "Very French. I'm sure the palace will love it."

She wasn't sure if his praise was genuine or sarcastic. Either way, it sent a pleasant thrill skittering through Aurélie. A pleasant thrill that irritated her to no end.

Why should she care what he thought about anything? Clearly he considered her spoiled. Foolish. Irresponsible. He'd said as much, right to her face. When he looked at her, he saw one thing. A princess.

She wondered what it would be like to be seen. *Really* seen. Every move she made back home was watched and reported. Not a day passed when her face wasn't on the front page of the Delamotte papers.

"Let's be serious, Mr. Drake. We both know I'm not going anywhere. You want that egg."

He took a few steps nearer, until she could feel the angry heat of his body. *Too close. Much too close.* "Yes, I do. But not as much as you wish to escape whatever it is you're running from. You're not going anywhere. I, on the other hand, won't hesitate to call the palace. Tell me, Princess, what is it that's got you so frightened?"

As if she would share any part of herself with someone like him. She hadn't crossed an ocean in an effort to get away from one overbearing man, only to throw herself into the path of another.

She leveled her gaze at him. "Nothing scares me, Mr. Drake. Least of all, your empty threats. If you're not prepared to uphold your end of our bargain, then I will, in fact, leave. Only I won't take my egg back to Delamotte. I'll take it right down the street to Harry Winston."

She pasted a sweet smile on her face. Dalton gave her a long look, and as the silence stretched between them, she feared he might actually call her bluff.

Finally, he placed a hand on the small of her back and said, "Come. Let's go home."

Chapter Four

The next morning, Dalton woke to the sensation of a warm body pressed against his. For a moment—just an aching, bittersweet instant—he allowed himself to believe he'd somehow traveled back to the past. Back to a time when there'd been more to life than work. And his office. And yet more work.

Then an unpleasant snuffling sound came from the body beside him, followed by a sneeze that sprayed his entire forearm with a hot, breathy mist. Dalton opened one eye. Sure enough, the beast he found staring back at him was most definitely not a woman. It was the damned dog.

He sighed. "What are you doing in here? I thought we agreed the bedroom was off-limits?"

The puppy's head tilted at the sound of his voice, a gesture that would have probably been adorable if the dog weren't so ridiculous-looking. And if he weren't currently situated in Dalton's bed, with his comically oversized head nestled right beside Dalton's on his pillow—eiderdown, imported from Geneva.

Dalton's gaze landed on a dark puddle of drool in the center of the pillowcase. Eiderdown or not, the pillow had just become a dog bed.

He rolled his eyes as he strode naked to the marble bathroom at the far end of the master suite and turned on the shower. Perhaps a soggy pillow was his penance for allowing a royal princess to sleep on his sofa rather than giving up his bed. Not that he hadn't tried. But at 1 a.m., she'd still been perched cross-legged on the oversized tufted ottoman in the living room, flipping through the hundreds of channels his satellite dish company offered, like a giddy child on holiday. Dalton hadn't even known he subscribed to so much programming. In fact, he couldn't remember the last time he'd turned on the television.

Sleeping in his office had become something of a habit, especially in recent years. But he couldn't very well spend the night there with Aurélie. He wasn't about to let the staff at Drake Diamonds see her hanging about his office in her pajamas. Explaining her sudden presence in his life—and the need for a duplicate key to his apartment—to the doorman of his building had been awkward enough. Until she'd slipped her arm through his and called him darling, that is.

They were masquerading as a couple. Again.

Dalton wasn't sure why he found that arrangement so vexing. She couldn't introduce herself as a princess. That was out of the question. Posing as his lover was the obvious choice.

Dalton stepped under the spray of his steam shower and let the hot water beat against the rigid muscles in his shoulders. Every inch of his body was taut with tension. He told himself it had nothing to do with the bewildered expression on the doorman's face as Aurélie had gripped his arm with her delicate fingertips and given him a knowing smile, as if they'd been on their way upstairs so he could ravish her. Was the idea of a woman in his life really so far-fetched?

Yes, he supposed it was. He didn't bring dates here. Ever. There were too many ghosts roaming the penthouse.

It isn't real. It's nothing but a temporary illusion, a necessary evil.

In just thirteen days, Dalton's existence would return to its predictable, orderly state. He'd have his life back. And that life would be significantly improved, because the display cases in the first floor showroom of Drake Diamonds would be filled with sparkling, bejeweled eggs.

He knew precisely where he would put the secret egg—in the same glass box that had once housed the revered Drake Diamond. The 130-carat wonder had held a place of honor in the family's flagship store since the day the doors opened to the public. Tourists came from all over the city just to see the stone, which had only been worn by two women in the 150 years since Dalton's great-great-great-great-great-grandfather had plucked it from a remote mine in South Africa and subsequently carved it into one of the most famous gemstones in the world.

The loss of that diamond just three months after the death of Dalton's father had been like losing a limb.

Granted, Artem had managed to buy it back for his wife, Ophelia. But it belonged to her personally now. Not the store. The Drake Diamond's display case sat empty.

Not that Dalton despised the sight of that vacant spot for sentimental reasons. The Drakes had never been an emotional bunch, and sentimentality had been the last thing on Dalton's mind once he'd learned he'd been passed over in favor of Artem for the CEO position. His pride was at stake. His position in the family business.

He didn't want to restore Drake Diamonds to its former glory. He wanted to surpass it, to make the institution into something so grand that his father wouldn't even recognize it if he rose from his grave, walked through the front door and set foot on the plush Drake-blue carpet.

Selling the Drake Diamond had been a necessity. Geoffrey Drake had plunged the family business so far into debt that there'd been no other option. And he hadn't told a soul. He'd sat in an office just down the hall from Dalton every day for years and hadn't said a word about the defunct diamond mine that had stripped the company of all its cash reserves. About the debt. About any of it.

Dalton shouldn't have been surprised. Honesty had never been his father's strong suit. Artem's very existence was a testament to their father's trustworthiness, or lack thereof. Dalton hadn't even known he had a brother until his father had brought five-year-old Artem home to the Drake mansion. Judging from the look of hurt and confusion on his mother's pale face, it had come as a surprise to her as well. Less than a year later, she was dead. To this day, Dalton's sister blamed their mother's death on a broken heart.

If there was a bright side to any of his family's sordid past or the recent sudden death of their patriarch, it was that the brothers had made peace with each other. At long last. When Artem had made the decision to sell the Drake Diamond, he'd saved the company. Dalton could admit as much.

But that didn't mean he had to like it.

He needed to be the one to transform Drake Diamonds into something more spectacular than it had ever been. It was the only way to justify his years of mindless devotion to the family business. He needed those years to mean something. He needed something to show for his life. Something other than loss.

He switched the shower faucet to the off position with more force than was necessary, and then grabbed a towel. On any other day, he would already have put in a solid hour behind his desk by now. He dressed as quickly as possible, adjusted the Windsor knot in his Drake-blue tie and resigned himself to the fact that it was time to venture into the living room and wake Aurélie. But first he needed to get the snoring beast out of his bed.

Dalton scooped the dog up and tried to wrap his mind around how something so tiny could make so much noise. Then his gaze landed on a wet spot in the center of the duvet. The little monster had peed in his bed. Perfect. Just perfect.

"Seriously?"

The animal's googly eyes peered up at Dalton. He sighed mightily.

"Aurélie!" He stormed into the living room without bothering to deal with the mess. "Your charge requires attention."

The television was blaring and the sofa was piled with

pillows and blankets, but Aurélie wasn't there. Dalton's temples began to pound. She'd run off? Again?

The puppy squirmed in his arms and let out a little yip, so Dalton lowered him to the floor. He scampered toward the kitchen, tripping over his own head a few times in the process.

"Mon petit chou!"

Dalton didn't know whether to feel relieved at the sound of Aurélie's voice or angry. Angry about the dog. About the near heart attack he'd just experienced when he'd thought she'd run off again. About every ridiculous thing she'd done since she'd breezed into his life less than twenty-four hours ago.

He settled on relief, until he followed the dog into the kitchen and caught his first glimpse of Aurélie's appearance.

She stood leaning against the counter with her mass of blond hair piled in a messy updo, wearing nothing but her luminous strand of gold pearls and a crisp men's white tuxedo shirt. His tuxedo shirt, if Dalton wasn't mistaken. But it wasn't the idea that she'd slept in his freshly pressed formal wear that got under his skin. It was the sight of her bare, willowy legs, the curve of her breasts beneath the thin white fabric of his shirt, the lush fullness of her bottom lip.

All of it.

He went hard in an instant, and the thought occurred to him that perhaps the only ghost inhabiting the apartment in the past few years had been him.

Whatever you do, don't take her to bed.

"Bonjour." Aurélie smiled. "Look at you, all dressed and ready for work. Why am I not surprised?"

Dalton shook his head. He was aroused to the point of pain. "We're not going to the office."

"Non?"

Non. Very much *non.* Suddenly, there was a more pressing matter that required attention—clothing the princess living under his roof before he did something royally stupid.

"Get ready. We're going shopping." He lifted a brow at the puppy in her arms. "As soon as you clean up after your dog."

After more cajoling than Aurélie could have possibly anticipated, Dalton finally acquiesced and agreed to take the subway rather than using his driver. He appeared distinctly uncomfortable doing so.

Aurélie couldn't help but wonder how long it had been since he'd ridden any form of public transportation. Granted, he was rich. That much was obvious. And just in case it hadn't been so glaringly apparent, the Google search Aurélie had conducted of Drake Diamonds on her phone the night before had confirmed as much.

According to *Forbes*, the flagship store on the corner of Fifth Avenue and 57th Street was the most valuable piece of real estate in the entire country. The building and its contents were worth slightly more than Fort Knox, where America's official gold reserves were held.

So yes, Dalton Drake was quite wealthy. And as he took such pleasure in pointing out over and over again, he was also busy. But this was New York. She'd assumed that everyone rode the subway, even rich workaholics like Dalton Drake.

Aurélie was also tempted to ask him how long it had been since he'd set foot in a building that didn't bear his name. She couldn't help but notice the discreet script lettering spelling out *The Drake* on the elegant black awnings of his apartment building. He seemed to spend every waking moment inside his sprawling penthouse or his jewelry store, where the name *Drake* was splashed everywhere, including across the structure's granite Art Deco exterior.

She didn't ask him either of those things, though. Instead, she soaked up every detail of riding the city's underground—the click of the silver turnstiles, the bright orange seats, the heady feeling of barreling through tunnels. The train sped from stop to stop, picking up and letting off people from all walks of life. Students with backpacks. Mommies with infants. Businessmen with briefcases.

None of those businessmen, however, were quite as formidable as the man standing beside her. No matter how much she tried to ignore him, Aurélie was overly conscious of Dalton's presence.

As fascinated as she was by the hordes of New Yorkers, the bustling subway stations, even the jostling movement of the train, she couldn't fully focus on any of it. Her gaze kept straying to Dalton's broad shoulders, his freshly shaven square jaw, his full, sensual mouth.

If only she could ignore him properly. But it proved an impossible task, no matter how hard she tried. During the frantic disembarking process at one of the stops, someone shoved Aurélie from behind and she found herself pressed right up against Dalton's formidable chest, her lips mere inches from his. She stiffened, unable to move or even breathe, and prayed he couldn't feel the frantic beating of her heart through the soft cashmere of his coat.

She'd been so overwhelmed by the sheer closeness of him that she couldn't quite seem to think, much less right herself. Until he glared down at her with that disapproving gray gaze of his. *Again.*

Right. He was a serious CEO, and she was nothing but a spoiled, irresponsible princess. Duly noted.

"We're here," he said, as the doors of the train whooshed open.

Aurélie glanced at the tile mosaic sign on the wall. *Lexington Avenue.* "Wait, this isn't…"

But Dalton's hand was already in the small of her back and he was guiding her through the station and out onto the snowy sidewalk before she could finish her thought. As usual, he was on a mission. Aurélie was just along for the ride, but at least when he noticed how enraptured she was by the opulent shop windows, he slowed his steps. When she stopped to admire a display of dresses made entirely of colorful paper flowers, she caught a glimpse of Dalton's reflection, and it looked almost as though he were smiling at her.

Then their eyes met in the glittering glass and any trace of a smile on his handsome face vanished as quickly as it had appeared.

He cleared his throat. "Shall we continue?"

That voice. Such a dark, low sound that sent a dangerous chill skittering up Aurélie's spine, for which she heartily admonished herself. She shouldn't be attracted to Dalton Drake. She couldn't. He had too much leverage over her as it was. Besides, she had enough men in her life. More than enough.

"Yes." She breezed past him as if she knew precisely where they were headed, when in fact, she hadn't a clue. "Let's."

"Aurélie," he said, with a hint of amusement in his tone. "We're going that way."

He pointed over his shoulder. This time, he most definitely smiled, and his grin was far too smug for Aurélie's taste.

Fine, she thought. No, not fine. Good. He was much easier to despise when he was being arrogant. Which, to Aurélie's great relief, was most of the time.

They walked the next few blocks in silence until they reached a sleek black marble building that appeared to take up an entire city block. Like both of Dalton's name-sake buildings, it had a doorman stationed out front. And gold-plated door handles. And a glittering, grand chandelier Aurélie could see through the polished windows. She squinted up at the sign. *Bergdorf Goodman.*

Without even setting foot inside, she could tell it was elegant. Tasteful. Expensive. Everything she didn't want.

She shook her head. *"Non."*

Beside her, Dalton sighed. "I beg your pardon?"

Aurélie pretended not to notice the hint of menace in his deep voice. "No, thank you. I'd rather go some-place else."

"But we haven't even gone inside." He eyed her.

Let him be mad. Aurélie didn't care. The rest of her life would be spent in designer dresses and kitten heels. This was *her* holiday, not his. She had no intention of spending it dressed like a royal. "I don't need to go in. I can tell it's not the sort of place where I want to shop for clothes."

The doorman's gaze flitted toward them. He'd looked utterly bored as they approached, but now his expression was vaguely hopeful. She realized he probably thought she and Dalton were a couple in the midst of some sort of domestic squabble.

Dalton lowered his voice. "Aurélie, you need clothes. This building is full of them. Dresses, blouses, pants." He cast a pointed glance at her legs. "Pajamas."

Pajamas?

So that's what this oh-so-urgent shopping spree was about. Dalton had been so horrified to find her wearing his tuxedo shirt this morning that he'd felt the need to cancel all his plans for the day and drag her to this fancy, impersonal department store.

She dropped all attempts at civility. "I'm not going in there, Mr. Drake."

Aurélie might not be American, but she'd seen *Pretty Woman.* Several times, actually. She knew precisely what would happen if she followed him inside the boutique. She'd walk out an hour from now looking like a princess from head to toe.

He crossed his arms and stared at her for a moment that stretched on too long. "May I ask why not?"

Intense much?

She felt breathless all of sudden, much to her annoyance. "I have no desire to play the part of Julia Roberts to your Richard Gere."

His broad shoulders shifted. Not that Aurélie was looking at them, because she wasn't. Not intentionally anyway. "I have no idea what you're talking about."

Of course he didn't. The man had probably never watched a movie in his life. Or done anything else fun, for that matter. "I'd prefer to go somewhere else. A vintage shop, perhaps?"

"A vintage shop?" He laughed, but somehow didn't

sound the faintest bit amused. "You're royalty and you want to wear a dead person's discarded clothes?"

"Yes. I do, even though you seem to be doing your best to make it sound disgusting."

Aurélie quite liked the idea of browsing through a vintage shop. She'd never shopped at one before, never even seen one. It sounded like fun. Or it would have, if she hadn't been accompanied by the world's most surly escort. "Come now, Mr. Drake. You and I both know you have a fondness for old treasures."

Like imperial jewels.

She very nearly said it, but she didn't have to.

"Fine, but we're taking a town car this time." He stalked to the curb, lifted an arm and a sleek black sedan materialized within seconds. Naturally. Even the traffic in New York obeyed his orders.

"After you." He held the door open.

"Merci." Aurélie climbed inside. "So where are we going?"

"Williamsburg. That's in Brooklyn," he clarified in his usual stiff tone.

The driver must have overheard, because they soon began a slow crawl across Manhattan. Aurélie had never seen such crowded streets in her life. In Delamotte, the major highway wrapped around a seaside cliff. More people drove mopeds than cars. There were sea breezes and salt air. Here, there were bike messengers zipping between automobiles, musicians on street corners and people selling things in stalls on the sidewalk—newspapers, purses, winter hats and gloves.

She felt suddenly as if she were in the center of everything and the whirling snow, the people and the cars with their blaring horns were all part of some mysterious, magnificent orbit.

So much life, so much movement—it made her giddy. A person couldn't stand still in a place like this, and Aurélie had been doing just that for such a very long time. All her life, it seemed.

"It's wonderful, isn't it?" she whispered with an awe-struck tremble to her voice.

Dalton regarded her closely. Curiously. "What's wonderful?"

"This." She waved a hand toward the scene outside the car windows, where dizzying snow fell on the beating heart of the city. "All of it."

Dalton looked at her for a beat too long. Long enough for her cheeks to grow warm. Without taking his eyes off her, he spoke to the driver. "Pull over, please."

The driver's gaze flitted to the rearview mirror. "Here, sir? We're only halfway to Brooklyn."

"Yes, I know," Dalton said. He knocked on the window and pointed at something outside. Aurélie wasn't sure what. There was so much to look at, so much to take in. She didn't know where to look first.

He glanced at Aurélie. "Stay here. I'll be right back."

He was *leaving*? Unbelievable.

"Wait. Where are you going?" Had he sensed a diamond emergency somewhere? Had the store run out of those little blue boxes? She placed a hand on his forearm.

He looked at her fingertips gripping the sleeve of his coat and then met her gaze. "Let go, Aurélie. And for once in your life, could you please do as I say and stay here? I'll be back momentarily."

She released his sleeve and crossed her arms. What was she doing, grabbing him like that anyway? Dalton was free to go wherever he liked. She'd actually prefer to spend the rest of the day on her own. Of course she would. "Fine."

In a flash, he climbed out of the car and shut the door behind him. A flurry of snowflakes blew inside the cab and danced in the air, as soft as feathers. Aurélie watched them drift onto the black leather seat and melt into tiny puddles. And for an odd, empty moment, she felt acutely alone.

She felt like crying all of a sudden, and she didn't even know why.

Aurélie exhaled slowly, willing the tears that had gathered in her eyes not to fall. What was wrong with her? This was what she wanted. Adventure. Independence. Freedom. All the things her mother had never experienced.

She reached for her Birkin, removed her iPhone from the interior pocket and slipped the SIM card back inside. Now seemed as good a time as any to check her messages and see who all had figured out she'd gone missing.

The phone seemed to take forever to power up and once it finally did, the display didn't show a single voice mail message. Nor any texts.

That couldn't be right, could it?

While she was staring at the little screen, the phone rang, piercing the silence of the backseat. It startled her so much that she nearly dropped it.

She took a deep breath and closed her eyes.

Maybe it was Dalton. Maybe he was calling to apologize for running off. *Not likely.* Deep down, she knew it couldn't be him. The only people who had anything to say to her were on the other side of the world.

She opened her eyes. A glimpse of the display confirmed her deepest fears. *Office of Royal Affairs*. Her private secretary.

The palace was looking for her. Aurélie's heart beat against her rib cage like a wild bird caught in a net. She peered out the window in search of Dalton, but the city had swallowed him up.

She cleared her throat, pressed the talk button and very nearly answered in English, which would have been a massive red flag. *Focus. "Allô?"*

"Bonsoir, Your Royal Highness." *Bonsoir. Good night.* It was already evening in Delamotte, which made it seem somehow farther away, only not quite far enough. "Do you have a moment to go over your schedule for the rest of the week?"

"My schedule?" Aurélie swallowed. What was happening? Had her own staff not even realized she was missing yet? "Of course."

"As we discussed last week, Lord Clement will be coming to the palace the day after tomorrow to take your picture. The Reigning Prince would like a new photo for the impending press release."

Aurélie's stomach churned. *Breathe. Just breathe.* Lord Clement was the official royal photographer, one of her father's oldest and dearest friends.

"The day after tomorrow isn't a good day." *Since I'm 4,000 miles away and everything.* "We need to reschedule, *s'il vous plaît."*

"I'm afraid we can't, Your Royal Highness. The press announcement is scheduled for next Friday."

Aurélie felt like she might be sick all over the backseat. She'd thought if she left Delamotte she could slow things down somehow. She'd only been gone a day and a half, and already she felt different.

But nothing had really changed, had it? They hadn't even realized she'd gone. She might be in America, but her life in Delamotte was still proceeding as planned. With or without her.

"Your sitting with Lord Clement is scheduled for 4:00 in the afternoon in the state ballroom. The Reigning Prince would like you to wear the gold brocade dress and the Marchand family tiara." Because apparently, although Aurélie was a grown woman, she wasn't allowed even the simple freedom of choosing her own clothes.

Her throat grew tight. "I understand."

"*Trés bien.* I'll phone Lord Clement and tell him you've confirmed. *Au revoir.*"

The line went dead before Aurélie could respond. She sat staring at the darkened phone in the palm of her hand. Dread fell over her in a thick, suffocating embrace.

What have I done?

Her escape may have gone unnoticed by royal staffers thus far, but failing to show up for a sitting with Lord Clement most definitely would not. Every royal office in Delamotte would hear about it. As would her father. And possibly even the press. Her face would be on the front page of every newspaper on the French Riviera, beneath the headline *Runaway Princess*.

Her heart lurched. But it wasn't too late, was it? If she caught a plane tomorrow, she could be standing in the ballroom with the Marchand family tiara anchored to her head within forty-eight hours. Then next week, she would be headline news for a different reason altogether.

She powered down her phone and removed the SIM card again. Although she wasn't even sure why she bothered. She should go home. Leaving hadn't changed anything. Not really. Staying in New York wouldn't, either. She couldn't outrun her destiny. Believing that she could was just a naïve, reckless mistake. Her mother hadn't been able to escape, and neither could she.

The car door opened, and suddenly Dalton was back inside the car in a flurry of snow and frosty wind. He slid in place beside her, holding a tissue-wrapped bundle. Aurélie tried her best to focus on him without really looking at him. She couldn't face him. Not after the phone call.

She was confused enough as it was without having to worry about what he'd have to say if she turned tail and ran back home. After everything she'd put him through— the disappearing, the dog, the constant arguing—he'd be furious. Or quite possibly relieved. Aurélie wasn't sure which she preferred.

"Look at me," he ordered. He cupped her face and forced her to meet his gaze. "Aurélie, is something wrong?"

Yes. Everything is wrong.

"No." She smiled her perfectly rehearsed princess smile, slid her cell phone back inside her purse and concentrated all her efforts on keeping her tears at bay.

But she felt his gaze on her, hot and penetrating. She couldn't look him the eye. She just couldn't. If she did, the truth would come tumbling out of her mouth. All of it. Her father's plans. The looming palace announcement. If she said the words aloud, they would feel real. And she so desperately needed to believe they weren't.

Just a little bit longer.

She focused instead on the knot in his Drake-blue tie. "Where have you been?"

"Getting this for you." He handed her the tissue-wrapped bundle. It warmed her hands.

Aurélie's defenses dropped, and she stared at him in disbelief. "You bought me a gift."

He frowned, which in no way diminished the potency of his chiseled good looks. "No, I didn't."

She looked at the plain white package in her lap and then back up at Dalton. He seemed nearly as surprised by this strange turn of events as she was. "Yes, you did."

He rolled his eyes. "Don't get too excited. Trust me. It's nothing."

She couldn't imagine what it could be, but something told her it meant more than Dalton was letting on. He wasn't the kind of man to waste time with frivolity.

With great care, she peeled back the tissue. When she realized what he'd done, she couldn't seem to utter a word. She blinked to make sure what she was seeing was real—a hot dog. He'd gotten her a hot dog.

"It's a metaphor." He shrugged as though he were right, as if this silly little gesture meant nothing at all, when to Aurélie, it meant everything. "With mustard."

She didn't fully understand what happened next. Maybe she wasn't thinking straight after getting the call from the palace. Maybe the thought of going back home had broken something inside her. Maybe she no longer cared what happened to her at all.

Because even though she knew it was undoubtedly the gravest mistake of her life, Her Royal Highness Aurélie Marchand tossed her hotdog aside, grabbed Dalton Drake by the lapels and kissed him as though she wasn't already engaged to another man.

Chapter Five

The engagement wasn't quite official, but the royal wedding was already scheduled to take place in just under three months at the grand cathedral in Delamotte. Top secret of course, until the palace made its big announcement in twenty days.

Not that Aurélie was keeping track of the days, exactly. On the contrary, she'd been trying rather aggressively not to think about her pending engagement at all. As it turned out, though, being married off to a man thirty years her senior, a man she'd yet to actually meet in person, was something she couldn't quite make herself forget. No matter how very hard she tried.

Kissing Dalton Drake, however, proved to be a powerful diversion. Frighteningly powerful. The moment Aurélie's lips came crashing down on his, the constant ache in her heart seemed to tear wide open. It was excruciating. And exquisite. She was aware of nothing but sensation. Sensation so sweetly agonizing that there wasn't room for a single thought in her head. How was it possible to feel so beautifully broken?

His mouth was cold from the snowstorm, his tongue like ice as it moved against hers. Deep. Devouring. Delicious. God, was this what kissing was supposed to be like? Because it wasn't close to anything Aurélie had experienced before. She couldn't seem to catch her breath. And were those whimpering noises echoing in the interior of the car actually coming from her?

She should have been embarrassed, but she didn't seem to be capable of feeling anything but longing. Longing as hard and bright as a diamond. She'd needed to be kissed like this. She'd needed it so badly.

No, she realized. She hadn't needed this. She'd needed *him*. Dalton Drake.

"Oh Aurélie," he whispered, his breath now warm and wonderful against her lips.

Then he slid his hands into her hair, cradling the back of her head, pulling her closer. Closer, until their hearts pounded against each other and she could no longer tell where hers ended and his began.

If her actions had caught Dalton off guard, he certainly didn't let it show. On the contrary, the way he went about ravishing her mouth gave her the very real sense that he'd been ready for this. Ready and waiting, for perhaps as long as Aurélie had been waiting for something like this herself. Maybe even longer.

But that couldn't be true. Dalton had made it clear he was merely tolerating her until the imperial eggs went on display. And that was okay, because she'd never be a real part of his life, and he would never be part of hers. Nothing about her time in New York was real.

The kiss sure felt real, though. More than the crown on her head or the white dress she'd slip over her head in less than a month. *This is what life is supposed to be like,* she thought. *This* was passion. Raw. Bold. Blazing hot.

And wrong. So very, very wrong.

Would her husband ever kiss her like this? Would he twirl her gold pearls around his fingertips and use them to pull her into his lap like Dalton was doing? Would she thrill at the press of his erection through their clothes as she sat astride him? Would she have to stop herself from reaching for his zipper and begging him to enter her in the backseat of a town car in full view of the driver and all of greater Manhattan?

No.

Despite her staggering level of inexperience in the bedroom, Aurélie knew how rare this connection was. She sensed it. And as surely as she sensed it, she knew that no man's lips would ever touch her like this again. No other man would kiss her like she was a gemstone, cool and shimmering. A precious object that had been buried somewhere dark and deep, waiting for a kiss of perfect heat to bring her volcanic heart to the surface. Only this man. Only this place and time.

Dalton deepened the kiss, groaned into her mouth and Aurélie's head spun with the knowledge that he wanted her. She wrapped her fingertips around the smooth blue silk of Dalton's tie, anchoring herself in the moment before it slipped away.

What would he say if he knew? What would he think when he picked up the newspaper after she went back to Delamotte and saw her photograph alongside an older man who was her fiancé? How would he feel watching her on television stepping out of a glass coach on her wedding day? He would be furious. It would confirm every notion he'd ever had that she was spoiled, reckless and irresponsible.

At least, she hoped that was how he would feel. Fury she could handle. What she couldn't bear from Dalton was pity. She'd grown quite fond of the way he looked at her as if she were some rare exotic bird instead of a grown woman living under her father's thumb. Of course, those moments were heavily punctuated with looks of complete and utter exasperation. But every so often, when he turned his gray gaze on her, she felt herself blooming from the inside out. Like a peony unfolding before the dazzling heat of the summer sun in a tremulous display of flowering fragility.

He saw *her*. That was the difference. She didn't have to hide who she was when she was with Dalton Drake. For all the secrets she was keeping from him, he saw her for who she really was. Which was more than she could say for the entire kingdom of Delamotte.

She really should have seen the engagement coming. Women in her position had been subjected to arranged marriages since the beginning of time. But she'd been so blissfully naïve about her circumstances, she'd had no idea that something so archaic and demeaning could actually touch her perfect life.

If Aurélie hadn't found her mother's diary the day after her funeral, she would have never known the truth. Sometimes she wished she'd never opened that book and flipped through its gilt-edged pages. Then she might still believe the fairy tale, when in reality, her parents had never loved each other. Her father had one mistress after another, while her mother had no one. Theirs had been a marriage of convenience, a carefully arranged bargain of politics and power.

Now Aurélie's would be, as well.

She squeezed her eyes shut tight, and with each breath, each touch of her lips, she begged Dalton to make it stop. To somehow change the course of her future so she could always be this girl, this bold woman who could write her own destiny.

Please. Please. Please.

"Please..."

Oh God, had she really just said that out loud?

"Not here, darling. Not here." Dalton's voice was little more than a sigh, but it carried just enough of a reprimand to bring her back to her senses.

She opened her eyes and found him staring at her with an intensity that left her painfully vulnerable. Exposed. Ashamed. *Not here.* She looked down at herself and couldn't believe what she saw—her thighs straddling his lap, her hands on the solid wall of his chest, her lipstick smeared all over his mouth. What was she *doing*?

She'd all but begged him to make love to her when he'd shown no interest in her whatsoever. Actually, she may have even begged.

"Oh my God." She pulled away, horrified.

Then she heard a snap, like the sound of something breaking in two. For an odd moment, she was sure it was her heart. Until she realized her pearls were still twirled around Dalton's fingertips. Not the whole strand...only half of them. The remaining pearls were falling from her neck, one by one, dripping into Dalton's lap.

Aurélie gasped and her hand flew to her throat.

Dalton cursed, slid out from beneath her and started

chasing the gold pearls around the moving car, gathering them in his hands. But they rolled everywhere, as if refusing to be captured.

Aurélie remembered reading somewhere that pearls were a symbol of sadness and that each bead of a string of pearls represented a teardrop. She'd never given much thought to the legend before, but now she couldn't quite shake the idea of her mother's tears spilling all over the car. Lost.

What a mess she'd made of things.

By Dalton's best guess, he had $50,000 worth of South Sea pearls rolling around his feet…give or take a few thousand. The fact that Aurélie's priceless broken necklace was the least of his problems at the moment spoke volumes about the magnitude of the mistake he'd just made.

What the hell was going on? Had he seriously just had a make-out session with a princess in the backseat of a hired car while a total stranger drove them across the Brooklyn Bridge? Yes. Apparently, he had. And judging by the magnitude of the erection straining his fly, he'd quite enjoyed it.

But now…

Now Aurélie was looking around with a dazed expression on her face, her eyes shiny with unshed tears. Shell-shocked. Horrified.

Meanwhile, the driver kept shooting glances in the rearview mirror while Dalton crawled all over the car trying to save the pearls. Who knew it was possible for a simple kiss to cause this much mayhem?

Who are you kidding, you idiot? There was nothing simple *about that kiss.*

He sat up and poured a handful of pearls into his pocket. "I'm sorry, Aurélie."

God, was he ever sorry.

Dalton had done the one thing he'd promised himself he wouldn't do. Granted, he hadn't slept with her. But what he'd done might have been worse. They were in a public place. Anyone could see them through car windows. Not to mention the chauffeur!

What if the driver recognized him? What if the driver recognized *her*? There were more things wrong with this scenario than there were pearls bouncing around the car.

"No, it was my fault. I shouldn't have…" Aurélie bit her pillowy bottom lip, and Dalton had to look away to stop himself from pillaging her rosy mouth all over again.

"I'm the one who's sorry." Dalton let out a strained exhale and focused on the pearls. If he met Aurélie's gaze for even a second, surely she'd see the truth written all over his face—it had taken every last shred of self-control to stop things when he did. Part of him wondered how he'd managed it.

Please. There'd been a world of promise in that sweet whisper. Promise that taunted him now, like the perfume of hyacinths left hanging in the air after a lucid fever dream. And now every heartbeat was a knife to his ribs. His hands shook so hard he couldn't manage to piece together the necklace. Pearls kept slipping through his fingers.

Please. That word would haunt him for a thousand sleepless nights to come, which in a way would be a painful relief. He'd grown altogether weary of the regret that had been his only bedtime companion since the night Clarissa died.

He hadn't been in love with Clarissa. He'd realized that in the years since her passing. Perhaps he'd known as much all along. He'd cared about her, of course. He never would have asked her to marry him if he hadn't, despite the expectations of both their families. But his feelings for Clarissa had been closer to the brotherly affection he felt for Diana than romantic love.

If he'd felt differently, he would have picked up the phone that night. He would have been home instead of sitting behind his desk. Clarissa would still be alive, and he wouldn't be situated in the back of a car with his thigh pressed against Aurélie's, wanting, *needing*, to touch her. Kiss her. Taste her.

He blamed himself. Not just for Clarissa—that was a given. But the responsibility for what had just happened with Aurélie also rested squarely on his shoulders. He wanted her. He'd wanted her since the moment he'd seen the hope that shone in her eyes. Hope like emerald fire.

That first day in his office, she'd turned her aching eyes on him as the glittering egg sat between them. And the force of her yearning had nearly knocked him out of his chair.

Desire. It had shimmered in the air like diamond dust. He hadn't known what it was she wanted so badly. He still didn't. But that ache, that need, had kindled something inside him. He'd been numb for so long that he couldn't remember what it was like to feel, to want, to need.

One look at Aurélie had been enough to conjure a memory. His life hadn't always been this way. He'd felt things once. What might it be like to feel again?

Dalton had no idea. All he knew was that he wanted to consume Aurélie, to devour her, until he figured it out. He wanted to want the things she wanted, to feel the things she felt—life, longing.

Love.

No. Not love. Anything *but love.*

He wasn't wired that way. He wasn't capable of love. Hadn't history proved as much? He had even less to offer now, after the way he'd failed Clarissa. She'd deserved better. So did Aurélie. And Dalton refused to be like his father. He wouldn't be the kind of man who did nothing but take.

Take, take, take.

He stared ahead. He couldn't bring himself to look at Aurélie quite yet. He couldn't bear to see the heat in her gaze, the light that radiated from her as if she were a brilliant-cut ruby. Not now. Not while the taste of her scarlet lips still lingered on his tongue.

If he did, there'd be no stopping this time. Not until he'd plunged himself fully inside her and felt her exquisite body shuddering beneath him.

The city whirred past them in a blur of snow, steel and melancholy gray. Dalton breathed in and out, clenching his hands into fists in his lap. He'd let himself slip. He wouldn't do so again. Aurélie was off-limits, and besides, he was comfortable with his life now. His orderly, predictable life.

But despite every effort to regain control, to slide back into a state of numbness, he couldn't seem to still the incessant pounding of his pulse. *Please. Please. Please.*

Chapter Six

Dalton was behind his desk at Drake Diamonds the next morning before the sun came up. He'd left instructions with the doorman to arrange for a driver to bring Aurélie to the store whenever she liked. Granted, leaving her alone for any length of time was a risk, given her penchant for running away. But nothing seemed as dangerous as it would have been for Dalton to play house with her all morning.

Aurélie had come home with piles of eclectic clothing from their trip to Williamsburg, but not a single pair of pajamas. After the disastrous car ride, Dalton couldn't take watching her move about his apartment in his tuxedo shirt again. He just couldn't. Another glimpse of her willowy porcelain legs stretching from beneath the bottom of his own shirt while she peered up at him with those luminous emerald eyes of hers would have been more than his suddenly overactive libido could take. He was only human.

He and Aurélie had danced carefully around each other for the remainder of the day. At the vintage shop, she'd disappeared behind dressing room curtains with one colorful outfit after another, but never came out to model anything.

Dalton told himself that was fine. For the best, really. But he hadn't realized how much he would have liked seeing her twirl in front of the shop's floor-to-ceiling mirrors until he'd found himself relegated to a purple velvet chair in the corner. Alone. And more sexually frustrated than he'd ever been in his life.

How had his life gotten so absurdly complicated in the span of just a few days?

Enough was enough. He couldn't live like this. He wouldn't. He had work to do. Loads of it. He should be busy confirming the arrangements for the upcoming gala or working on the spring advertising campaign. Instead he was flipping through a stack of tabloids, praying he wouldn't stumble on a photo of himself ravishing Aurélie in the back of a car.

There was a knock on his office door, and before Dalton could stash his pile of newspapers, Artem poked his head inside.

"Good morning, brother." His gaze dropped to the copy of *Page Six* spread open on Dalton's desk. "Interesting reading material."

God help Dalton if he and Aurélie had been caught on film. He'd never hear the end of it. "Good morning." He flipped the paper closed and waved Artem inside.

His brother clicked the door shut behind him. "I was wondering if you were going to show up today. When you didn't turn up yesterday, I assumed you were on your deathbed or something. I can't recall when you've ever missed a day of work before. You know we have Diana's horse show in the Hamptons tomorrow, don't you?"

"Of course I do." Dalton sighed.

He'd actually forgotten about his sister's event. That would mean more time away from the store, and he'd just missed nearly two full days of work because he'd been tied up with Aurélie.

He'd never been away from the office for two consecutive days before. Ever. He'd even managed to put in a solid eight hours the day of Clarissa's funeral. It had made perfect sense at the time, but now he wasn't so sure.

Nothing made much sense at the moment.

"Have a seat. I need to discuss something with you." He shoved the tabloids in a drawer so Artem wouldn't be prompted to mention them again. Dalton would have been quite happy to forget them himself.

"Sure. I'm glad you're here. I wanted to ask you…" Artem's voice trailed off.

Dalton looked up to find him staring at Jacques who was curled in a ball on the sofa in the corner of the office. "Am I seeing things, or is that a puppy?"

He rolled his eyes. "Don't ask."

"Oh, I'm asking." Artem shook his head and let out a wry laugh. "I've known you since I was five years old, and somehow I missed the part about you being an animal lover. When did you get a dog?"

Dalton aimed an exasperated glance at Jacques, who responded by panting and wagging his entire backside. The dog was obsessed with him. The pup had responded to the pet sitter Dalton had hired the day before with overwhelming nonchalance. But he worshipped Dalton. Just his luck. "I didn't."

Artem sank onto the sofa beside Jacques and rested a hand on the little dog's back. Jacques went into an ecstatic fit of snuffling sounds as he shuffled toward his lap. "Then where did this sweetheart come from?"

Dalton cleared his throat. "He belongs to Aurélie."

Jacques flopped onto his back. The minute Artem started rubbing his belly, the puppy's tongue lolled out of the side of his mouth. A long string of drool dripped onto the sofa cushions. Naturally. "And he's at work with you because..."

"He likes me. God knows why. The feeling is definitely not mutual." The puppy was a walking train wreck. And constantly underfoot. Dalton could barely walk across the room without tripping over him, but his presence at Drake Diamonds pretty much guaranteed Aurélie would eventually show up. She'd never run off without her *petit chou.* "The homely little thing has hijacked my bed and destroyed half the pillows in my apartment."

"Your apartment?" Artem lifted a brow. "Does this mean Aurélie's staying with you?"

"It does." Dalton shrugged to indicate his nonchalance, but the gesture felt disingenuous. Forced.

Artem's gaze narrowed. "Let me see if I've got the facts straight here. You haven't been at work for a day and a half, Aurélie is living with you and you're letting her puppy—whom you clearly dislike—eat your furniture and slobber all over your office."

Sounds about right. "I realize how this looks."

"Do you really? Because it sort of looks like you're

sleeping with a runaway princess while you plan on exhibiting stolen royal jewels for your personal gain."

Dalton blinked. He'd never been on the receiving end of a lecture from his younger brother before. This was quite a role reversal, and it didn't sit well. Not at all.

"That's a gross representation of what's actually happening. For starters, she didn't steal the egg. She inherited it."

Artem stood and walked toward the desk, while Jacques grunted his displeasure at being left behind. "And do you think the palace will see it that way?"

Maybe. Maybe not.

He'd considered this complication, of course. But if things went as planned, the officials in Delamotte wouldn't know the egg was missing until its unveiling at the gala. By then, Drake Diamonds would be on the front page of every newspaper in the country. Mission accomplished. Aurélie would have a lot to answer for, but that wasn't his problem. Was it?

In retrospect, that attitude seemed rather harsh. When had he become his father?

Dalton swallowed. "Also, not that it's any of your business, but I'm not sleeping with her."

Artem looked down at him for a long, loaded moment.

Dalton hadn't slept with Aurélie. That much was true. It was also true that all he seemed to think about was how very much he wanted to take her to bed. Not wanted. *Needed.* He needed to feel the soft perfection of her curves beneath his palms once again, to feel the pulse at the base of her throat thundering at the touch of his lips, to hear that breathy whimper. *Please.*

Was it so obvious?

Judging by the look on Artem's face, yes. Apparently,

it was. "Look, do what you like with Aurélie. You're right. Whether or not you sleep with her isn't my business. Although, I can't help but mention that if I were sharing my home with the princess of a foreign principality whose most precious jewels are currently in the Drake Diamond vault, you'd have a few things to say about it."

Artem lifted a sardonic brow.

Dalton couldn't argue. He was right. And even though he had no intention of admitting as much to his younger brother, a line had most definitely been crossed.

He hadn't just crossed the line. He'd leaped right over it.

The way things stood, the two brothers had practically traded places, like they were in some third-rate comedy film.

Except Artem was married now, and he had a baby on the way. He was no longer the black sheep of the family. Apparently Dalton now held that title.

What kind of alternate reality was he living in? He was appalled at himself.

"You should probably know that while you were out of the office, you got a phone call." Artem sank into the wing chair on the opposite side of Dalton's desk. His uncharacteristically serious expression gave Dalton pause. "From the palace in Delamotte."

Great. Just great.

So they'd already found out. The palace officials knew about Aurélie. They probably even knew about the secret egg. His ambition, coupled with Aurélie's naïveté, had created an even more profound disaster than he'd anticipated.

He'd been an idiot to think he could get away with something like this. "How bad is it?"

Artem shrugged. "Not very. When Mrs. Barnes couldn't reach you on your cell, she came to me. I took the call."

When Mrs. Barnes couldn't reach you on your cell...

Memory hit Dalton hard and fast. Unexpected. Bile rose to the back of his throat, and he squeezed his eyes shut. But he could still see the notification on his phone. *Clarissa Davies, 19 Missed Calls.*

It wasn't as if he hadn't known. He'd seen the calls come rolling in, but he'd ignored them. Every last one.

Artem spoke again, his voice dragging Dalton mercifully back to the present. "Relax, brother. I handled it. Look, I know how you feel about your phone, but it's not a crime to miss a call."

"Don't go there, Artem," he said as evenly as he could manage. "Not now."

Artem held up his hands in a gesture of surrender. "Sorry. I know it's a difficult subject, but it's been six years. You don't have to be tethered to your phone twenty-four seven. Honestly, when Mrs. Barnes told me you weren't picking up, I was elated. I thought you'd actually gone and gotten yourself a life."

Dalton let out a bitter laugh. He didn't deserve a life. Not anymore. He probably never had, because he was a Drake through and through.

Like every other Drake man that had ever sat behind a desk, he was good at one thing: making money. Selling diamonds didn't leave much room for relationships, or for "a life" as Artem put it. Not the way the Drake men did it.

Dalton had tried it once, hadn't he? Never again. One dead fiancée was more than enough.

"It wasn't your fault, you know. She would have eventually found another time, another way," Artem said quietly.

They'd been over this before. The discussion was closed, as far as Dalton was concerned. What good could come of revisiting the past? Nothing. It wouldn't change a godforsaken thing. "Can we just cut to the chase? Tell me about the call."

Artem sighed. "They were calling to see if the eggs had arrived safely. It seems the palace courier, Monsieur Martel, still hasn't returned to work. There was some concern that he might have absconded with the royal jewels."

Dalton should have thought about this detail. He should have quizzed Aurélie about the courier before he'd even agreed to her terms. He was off his game. He'd been off his game since she'd walked through the door of his office. The time had come to get his head on straight again.

"What did you tell them?" he asked.

"I assured them the pieces for the exhibition had arrived, and the royal jewels were safely locked away in the Drake Diamond vault." Artem cleared his throat. "I failed to mention the treasure locked away in your apartment."

Glaring at his brother, Dalton exhaled.

Artem shrugged. "In all seriousness, have you thought about what you're going to do when they realize she's missing? Surely someone will notice."

Dalton's response rolled off his tongue before he even realized what he was saying. "With any luck, they won't before tomorrow. I'm putting Aurélie on a flight back to Delamotte tonight at midnight."

He'd been toying with the idea all morning, but hadn't realized he'd reached a decision until that precise moment. He'd known, though. He'd known all along that he should send her back. He should never have agreed to her silly plan in the first place.

Now he was just waiting. Waiting for her to show up so he could break the news that he was sending her away.

Dalton's gaze flitted to Jacques sleeping on the sofa, snoring loud enough to peel the Drake-blue paint off the walls. He frowned. What was to become of the dog? Surely she wouldn't leave the mutt behind.

Forget about the dog. This isn't about a dog.

It was about business, nothing more. At least that's what he'd been busy telling himself as he'd looked up the flight schedules to the French Riviera.

Artem leveled his gaze at Dalton. "What about the secret egg?"

"She can take it back with her. It's just not worth the risk." Something hardened inside Dalton. Something dark and deep. "Not anymore."

"What changed?"

Dalton grew still as memories moved behind his eyes in an excruciatingly slow, snow-laden waltz of wounded desire. He saw his fingers tangled in the silken madness of Aurélie's hair, her eyes glittering in the dark like the rarest of diamonds, her lips, bee-stung and bruised from his kisses as she pleaded with him for sweet relief. He saw pearls falling like teardrops, spilling into cupped hands faster than he could catch them.

What changed?

Everything.

Everything had changed.

He shrugged one shoulder and did his best to affect an indolent air. "I came to my senses. That's all."

Artem looked at him, long and hard. "You sure about this? Because I'll back you up, whatever you decide. We're a team, remember?"

All his life—from the time he'd barely been old enough to walk on the Drake-blue carpeting of the Fifth Avenue store, right up until the morning he'd listened to a lawyer recite the terms of his father's Last Will and Testament—Dalton had imagined himself running Drake Diamonds someday. Alone, not alongside his brother. Just him. Dalton Drake, Chief Executive Officer.

He'd never pictured himself as part of a team. Never wanted it. In reality, it wasn't so bad. One day, he might even grow accustomed to it.

"Absolutely." He nodded and gave his brother a genuine, if sad, smile. "I've made my decision. The princess is going back home where she belongs."

Aurélie should have been relieved to wake up alone in Dalton's pristine apartment. She still wasn't sure quite how to act around him after mauling him in the car.

What had come over her? She'd acted as if this person she'd been pretending to be in New York, this impulsive life she was leading, was actually real. It wasn't. Not at all. This was a holiday, nothing more.

But the holiday was clearly messing with her head. In a really big way.

She would have loved to blame her outlandish behavior on the hot dog. Or at the very least, the bearer of the hot dog.

She'd grown so accustomed to Dalton's straight-laced

businessman persona, that his simple act of kindness had caught her completely off guard. Every so often, he was soulful when she least expected it.

In those stolen moments of tenderness, she felt like she was seeing the real Dalton. The man behind the serious gray eyes and the Drake-blue tie. A man devastatingly beautiful in his complexity.

But really, how desperate did a girl have to be to throw herself at a man over a hot dog?

Sleep provided a temporary reprieve from Aurélie's mortification, but the moment her eyes drifted open, it all came crashing back—the cold fury of Dalton's lips, his wayward hands, the way he'd made her forget she was nothing but a virgin princess being married off to a complete and total stranger.

For one dazzling moment, she'd been more than that. She'd blazed bright, filled with liquid-gold, shimmering desire.

Until it was over.

Not here.

She'd felt herself disappearing again, falling away.

Maybe none of it had really happened. Maybe it had just been a bad dream. Aurélie's hand flew to her throat, hoping against hope that she'd find the smooth string of pearls still safely clasped around her neck, as she did every morning. But it wasn't. She found only her bare, unadorned neck beneath the open collar of Dalton's tuxedo shirt.

What was she still doing sleeping in that thing? The first night it had been a matter of necessity. It wasn't anymore.

But she liked waking up in Dalton's shirt. She liked the way his masculine scent clung to the fabric. She liked the way the cuffs skimmed the very tips of her finger-tips. She liked imagining him slipping it on sometime in the distant future and remembering a princess who lived on the other side of the world.

What was wrong with her? She had no business thinking such things. She was an engaged woman. Almost, anyway.

She sat up and glanced around the spacious living room in search of Jacques, but the little bulldog was nowhere to be seen. Aurélie sighed. He'd probably snuck his way into Dalton's bedroom again. Jacques seemed to be forming quite an attachment to the man, even though the infatuation was clearly one-sided. Aurélie would have probably found it amusing if it didn't remind her of her own nonsensical attachment to Dalton's shirt.

The bedroom was empty, of course. No dog. No Dalton.

On some level, she'd known. The air was calm, still. Void of the electricity that always seemed to surround him, like an electrical storm. He'd left a note in the kitchen with the number to call when she was ready for a driver to come round and pick her up. The note didn't say where the car would be taking her. It didn't have to.

Heigh-ho, heigh-ho, it's off to work we go.

Did the man do anything else?

Judging by the looks of his apartment, no. With its sleek lines and elegant white furniture, it was the epitome of moneyed simplicity. Tasteful. Pristine. But more than a tad sterile. After living there for a few days, Aurélie still marveled at the absence of photographs. There wasn't a single picture in the place. No candid snapshots, no family memories. It left her feeling strangely hollow. And sad for Dalton, although she knew she shouldn't.

He'd never given her the slightest indication he was unhappy with his station in life. On the contrary, he exuded more confidence than anyone she'd ever met.

She needed to get out of here, out of this apartment that felt so oddly unsettling without Dalton's brooding presence. Even if the car took her straight to the glittering store on Fifth Avenue. At least in Dalton's place of business, she would be less likely to accidentally kiss the stuffing out of him again. Before she went anywhere, though, she needed to check the news to make sure she still wasn't a headline.

Dalton's laptop was situated on the dining room table. Perfect. She could take a look at the US tabloids and then access the Delamotte papers online. She made a cup of coffee, sank cross-legged onto one of the dining room chairs and flipped open the computer. Then she nearly choked on her coffee when Dalton's screensaver came into view.

It was a photograph—a picture of a woman on horseback, and she was quite beautiful.

Aurélie stared at it until a sick feeling came over her. A sick feeling that seemed an awful lot like jealousy.

Oh, no. She slammed the computer closed. *This cannot be happening.* But it was. It *was* happening. She was jealous of a silly little screensaver, jealous over Dalton Drake.

She was in over her head. Whether she liked it or not, what had happened the day before changed things. She couldn't stay here. Not anymore. It was time to pack up her egg and go home.

She opened the laptop back up, steadfastly refused to allow herself even a glimpse at the pretty equestrian smiling at her from the screen and logged onto the internet. Within minutes, she'd booked herself on a commercial flight out of New York that would allow her to get back to Delamotte in time for her portrait session with Lord Clement the next day.

With any luck, by this time tomorrow she'd be back home, and it would be as though she'd never come to New York, never walked through snowy Central Park, never shopped for vintage clothes in Brooklyn. Never kissed Dalton Drake.

Her flight left at midnight. Now all she needed to do was get her egg back...

...and break the news to Dalton.

Chapter Seven

Aurélie dragged her feet for a good long while before leaving the apartment. She made a second cup of coffee and drank it while she watched the New Yorkers milling about on the crowded streets below. Steam rose up from the manhole covers, and snow covered everything, from the neat grid of sidewalks to the elegant spire of the Chrysler building towering over the Manhattan skyline. From above, the city looked almost like an old black-and-white movie—the kind she used to watch with her mother on late nights when her father was out on official crown business. Or so she'd thought.

She'd been so naïve. Naïve and happy. Ignorance really was bliss, wasn't it?

How different would things be right now if she'd never read her mother's journal? Would she be dreading her arranged marriage so much that she'd actually flee the country? Would she even be standing right here, right now, in Dalton Drake's quiet apartment?

Maybe.

Maybe not.

She almost wished she hadn't. Almost.

Stop. What's done is done.

She turned her back on the window and got down to the business of preparing to leave. She rinsed her coffee cup, put it in the dishwasher. She stripped the sofa of the sheets and blankets she'd been using, washed and dried them, then tucked them away in the massive walk-in closet in Dalton's master suite. All the while, she gave the dining room and Dalton's laptop a wide berth.

His closet was meticulously organized, of course. Even more so than her own closet at the palace. Unlike her walk-in, which was packed with gowns of every color under the sun, Dalton's was distinctly monochromatic. The spectrum ranged from sedate dove-gray and charcoal designer business suits to sleek black tuxedos. The sole splash of color was the selection of ties hanging side-by-side on two sections of wooden spools that flanked his full-length mirror. All the highest quality silk. All the same recognizable shade of blue.

Drake blue.

Aurélie shook her head. The man's identity was so tied to his family business that he didn't even own a single tie in a different hue. He took workaholic to a whole new level.

She found a small suitcase tucked away behind the wall of Armani and used it to pack her new vintage wardrobe. If Dalton balked, she'd arrange to send him a new one after she got home. It wasn't like he might need it between now and then. She doubted he'd even miss it. She wondered when he'd last taken a vacation. Then she reminded herself that Dalton Drake's vacation schedule was none of her concern.

I'll never see him again.

She froze. Swallowed. Then forced herself to take a deep breath.

Of course you won't see him again. That's the whole point of leaving.

It was for the best. The longer she stayed, the harder it would be to walk out the door. She'd already had a nonsensical fit of jealousy after seeing his screensaver. How much worse could things get if she stayed longer?

A lot worse. No question. Besides, if she didn't get on that midnight plane, she'd miss her portrait sitting. She was doing the right thing. The *only* thing. She'd run out of options.

She folded her new dresses with meticulous care and tried not to think about the fact that she'd probably never wear most of them. They were wholly inappropriate for royal life. But she couldn't dwell on that now. If she did, she might just fall apart. Anyway, she loved her new clothes. Maybe she'd get to wear them again…someday.

Keep busy. That's what she needed to do. Just stay as busy as possible between now and the time she needed to head to the airport.

When at last she'd erased every trace of her presence from the apartment, she asked Sam to fetch the driver. With only a matter of hours left before her flight, she couldn't put off the inevitable any longer. She had to tell Dalton she was leaving and demand that he return her egg.

As unpleasant as such a confrontation sounded, at least it would take place at the glittering store on Fifth

Avenue, where she wouldn't be tempted to repeat yesterday's mistake.

Of course she'd forgotten that making her way to Dalton's office would involve walking through the Engagements section on the tenth floor. Tightness gathered in her chest as the elevator doors slid open.

"Welcome." The elevator attendant's smile was too kind. Aurélie recognized him as the same man who'd witnessed her last near-panic attack.

Super. Even the elevator attendant pitied her. "Thank you," she said, and forced herself to put one foot in front of the other.

The showroom was even more crowded than it had been last time. A man wearing a Drake-blue bowtie walked past her holding a tray of champagne flutes. Couples sat, two by two, at each and every display case. One of the shoppers even had the word *Bride* spelled out in rhinestones on her white slim-fit tee.

Aurélie's mouth grew dry. *Bride.* She had trouble breathing all of a sudden. Even remaining upright seemed challenging. She swayed a little on her feet.

How many engaged couples could there possibly be in Manhattan?

"It's a little overwhelming, isn't it?" said someone beside her.

"Excuse me?" Aurélie turned to find a woman, blonde, graceful and judging by the size of her adorable baby bump, a few months pregnant.

"You must be Aurélie." She gave her a conspiratorial wink. "I'm Ophelia Drake, and believe me, I know how you feel."

Ophelia Drake—Artem's wife, Dalton's sister-in-law and the head jewelry designer for the company. Aurélie recognized her from the photo in the Drake Diamonds brochure she'd read in Dalton's office on her first day in New York.

What she hadn't gleaned from the brochure was how warm and open Ophelia Drake seemed. But nice as she appeared, she couldn't possibly know how Aurélie felt. No one could.

Upon closer inspection, something in the depths of Ophelia's gaze told Aurélie that she was no stranger to heartache. Interesting.

"Come with me. I know the perfect cure." Ophelia wrapped an arm around her waist and steered her through the maze of wedded bliss and down the hall. In the time it took to leave Engagements behind, Aurélie decided she quite liked Ophelia. She liked her a lot.

"Here we go. Grab a seat," Ophelia said, ushering her into a small room filled with sleek silver appliances, trays of champagne and at least ten or twelve plates of tiny cakes.

Aurélie looked around. "Is this a kitchen?"

Ophelia nodded and slid a plate of petit fours onto the table in front of Aurélie. "I used to hide in here sometimes." She waved a flippant hand toward Engagements. "When it got to be a little much out there, I'd sometimes sneak in here for some cake. This is where I met my husband, actually."

"Here in the kitchen?" Aurélie picked up a petit four, a perfect replica of the small Drake-blue boxes wrapped with white ribbon that customers carried home everyday. It looked too pretty, too perfect to eat.

"Yes. In this very spot." Ophelia frowned at the tiny cake in Aurélie's hand. "Are you going to eat that or just stare at it? Because I'm eating for two and if it sits there much longer, I can't promise I won't snatch it right out of your hand."

Aurélie laughed. It felt good to laugh. Right. Easy. She hadn't laughed much since she'd kissed Dalton. The past twenty-four hours or so had been spent mired in regret.

She smiled at Ophelia and popped the petit four in her mouth. "Oh. My. God. This is delicious."

Ophelia shrugged. "Told you. It's a wonder what just a little bite of cake can do sometimes."

Aurélie licked a crumb from her fingertip and shamelessly reached for another petit four. "Can I ask you something?"

"Sure." Ophelia leaned back in her chair and rested a hand on her belly the way blissful expectant mothers had a tendency to do.

She was a lovely woman. Aurélie remembered reading in the brochure that Ophelia's first designs for Drake Diamonds had been a dance-inspired collection because she used to be a ballerina. Her training showed. Even pregnant, she carried herself with the grace and poise of a former dancer.

But it wasn't her willowy limbs that made her beautiful, nor the elegance of her movements. It was the way she glowed. Ophelia was happy. Truly happy.

Aurélie couldn't help but feel a little envious. "Isn't Artem the CEO? How is it that you first met him here instead of on the sales floor?"

Ophelia's lips curved into a smirk. "Let's just say Artem wasn't always so serious about this place. It took a while for him to adjust to the role." She tilted her head and gave Aurélie a puzzled look. "I'm surprised Dalton hasn't mentioned it to you. You're staying with him, right? Artem's work habits used to bother him to no end."

"*Oui*. I'm staying with him. But we don't really talk much." *We just argue. And kiss. Then argue some more.* "I'm not sure if you've noticed, but Dalton isn't exactly the chatty type."

"Oh, I've noticed." Ophelia grew quiet for a moment. Pensive. "I've also noticed he seems a bit different since you arrived."

Aurélie sighed. "If he's been extra cranky, I'm afraid that's my fault. We rub each other the wrong way." A bigger understatement had never been uttered.

Ophelia's brow furrowed. "Actually, I was thinking the opposite."

Aurélie opened her mouth, and for a few prolonged seconds, nothing came out of it. *The opposite?* Meaning that she and Dalton somehow rubbed each other the *right* way? Impossible. No. Just…no.

Yet her heart gave a rebellious little lurch all the same.

She cleared her throat and reminded herself that in a matter of hours she'd be on an airplane headed halfway across the world. As she should. "I have no idea what you're talking about."

Ophelia smiled. "I'm talking about the dog in his office, for one thing."

Oh yes, that.

"And his scarcity around here the past few days. Dalton doesn't take time off. Ever." She shrugged. "Unless Diana has a horse show in the area, like she does tomorrow."

Aurélie's heart stuttered to a stop. So the horsewoman had a name. Diana.

Well whoever Diana was, Aurélie pitied her. She

couldn't imagine being in a relationship with a man who was so clearly addicted to his work, was pathologically allergic to fun and hated rescue puppies.

For some reason though, the storm of emotions brewing in Aurélie's soul felt very little like pity. She swallowed around the lump that had taken up swift residence in her throat. "I…um…" *Don't ask about Diana the horse lover. Do* not.

"Diana is Artem and Dalton's younger sister," Ophelia explained. "The third Drake."

"Oh, I see." It was ludicrous how delighted she sounded. Borderline thrilled. She prayed Ophelia didn't pick up on it.

Judging by her amused expression, she did. Mercifully, Artem strode into the kitchen before Ophelia could comment. He took one look at the empty plate in the center of the table and aimed a knowing grin at his wife. "Busted. Again."

Ophelia lifted a challenging brow. "I'm eating for two, remember?"

As Aurélie watched Artem bend to give his wife a tender kiss on the cheek, she was struck by how different he appeared from Dalton, despite the fact that they had similar aristocratic good looks. Same dark hair, same chiseled features. But Aurélie had grown so accustomed to the thunder in Dalton's gaze and the underlying intensity of his movements that witnessing Artem's casual elegance was like seeing the flip side of a silver coin.

"Sweetheart," Ophelia said. "Have you met Aurélie?"

Artem straightened and shook her hand. "Not officially, although I've heard quite a bit about you. It's a pleasure to meet you."

"Enchanté."

Meeting Dalton's family felt strange. She'd known Drake Diamonds was a family institution, but Dalton sure didn't seem much like a family man. Probably because he so obviously wasn't, the photograph on his laptop notwithstanding.

His sister.

Diana is Artem and Dalton's younger sister. The third Drake.

The woman's identity didn't change a thing. It didn't change the fact that she had no business kissing Dalton. And it most definitely didn't change the fact that Dalton had put an abrupt stop to her advances in the car. Or that she had a real life with real responsibilities on the other side of the world.

Which made the extent of her relief all the more alarming.

Where the hell is she?

Dalton checked the hour on his Cartier for what had to be the hundredth time. 8:45 p.m. Outside his office window, the sky had long grown dark. The store would be closing in less than fifteen minutes. Aurélie's plane was due to board in just under three hours, and he still hadn't managed to tell her she'd be on it.

He sighed mightily. According to Sam, she'd left the apartment building an hour ago. She should have breezed into his office by now, but of course, she hadn't. Dalton didn't know why he was surprised. Aurélie wasn't exactly a paragon of predictability. A rebellious spike of arousal shot through him, and he was forced to acknowledge that he found her lack of predictability one of her most intriguing qualities.

Too bad it also drove him batshit crazy.

By this time tomorrow, she'll be out of your life for good. He just had to make it through the next few hours and see that Aurélie got on the plane. Surely getting her strapped into a first-class airplane seat on time was a doable task. Of course, it would help if he knew where she was.

"What now?" Dalton groaned as he felt an all-too familiar nudge on his shin. He looked down to find Aurélie's dog staring up at him with its big, round googly eyes. Yet again. "You can't be serious."

The puppy pawed at him again and let out a pitiful whine. Dalton had already been forced to have Mrs. Barnes walk the blasted thing twice since lunchtime when he'd done the honors himself. There had also been an unfortunate accident on his office floor, evidenced by a wet spot on the Drake-blue carpet that belied the dog's small size. Tempted as Dalton was to ignore the persistent pawing on his shins, he knew better.

He buzzed his secretary's desk, but the call went unanswered. Which didn't come as much of a surprise since she'd been officially relieved of her duties at 6:00. Sometimes she stayed late in case Dalton needed any after-hours assistance, but he figured puppy-sitting didn't exactly fit into her job description.

"Fine," he muttered, scooping the tiny bulldog into the crook of his elbow. "Let's do this."

The dog buried his oversized head into Dalton's chest, made a few of the snuffling noises that Aurélie somehow found endearing and left a smear of god-knows-what in the middle of Dalton's tie.

Splendid. "Thanks for that," he muttered.

Jacques snorted in response. Dalton rolled his eyes and stalked down the hallway, intent on getting the business over with as swiftly as possible. But as he approached the kitchen, Jacques's sizeable ears pricked forward. His stout little body trembled with excitement, and when they reached the doorway, the reason for his elation came into view.

"Aurélie." Dalton stopped in his tracks.

There she was—sitting calmly at the kitchen table nibbling on petit fours like Marie Antoinette while her dog slobbered all over his Burberry suit. Why hadn't he been notified of her arrival? And why were Artem and Ophelia chatting her up like the three of them were old friends?

"You're late," he said without prelude or ceremony.

Artem cleared his throat.

"How is that possible when I don't even work here?" Aurélie popped the remaining bit of cake in her mouth, affording Dalton a glimpse of her cherry pink tongue, a view that aroused him beyond all reason.

She made no move to stand, instead remaining regally seated in her chair wearing one of the vintage dresses she'd chosen the day before—pale blue with a nipped in waist, voluminous skirt and large white polka dots. Wholly inappropriate for winter in New York, yet undeniably lovely. Dalton found himself wishing the dress were a shade or two darker. He'd like to have seen her dressed in Drake blue. His color...

His.

Mine. The word pulsed in his veins with a predatory fervor.

He needed to get her out of his store, his life and back to Delamotte where she belonged. The fact that she'd yet to so much as look at him, focusing instead on the squirming puppy in his arms, did nothing to suppress his desire. Much to his frustration.

The ways in which she vexed him were innumerable. He smiled tightly. "Apologies, Your Highness. I forget that work—or responsibility of any kind—is a foreign concept for you."

When at last she met his gaze, thinly veiled fury sparkled in the depths of her emerald eyes.

"Okay, then," Artem said with forced cheerfulness. "It's getting rather late. I need to get my pregnant wife home. We'll give you two some privacy, because don't you have something you need to discuss with Aurélie, Dalton?"

Artem shot Dalton a loaded glance.

"Is that right?" Aurélie stood, and the folds of her pale blue skirt swirled around her shapely legs. "I have something to discuss with you as well. Something important."

"Very well." Dalton nodded. "But at the moment, your dog requires attention. Shall we?"

She reached for Jacques, and the dog went into a spastic fit of delight. Dalton was all but ignored, which should have been a relief. The fact that he felt the opposite was every bit as mystifying as it was infuriating.

He smoothed down his dampened tie and waited as Aurélie gathered the puppy in her arms and walked past him, out the door. He glanced at his brother and sister-in-law, still sitting at the kitchen table, looking mildly amused. "Good night, Ophelia. Artem." He nodded.

Artem arched an expectant brow, but said nothing. He didn't need to. Dalton got the message loud and clear. The time had come to tell Aurélie she was leaving. It was now or never.

Chapter Eight

Aurélie's hands were shaking. Thank goodness she could hide them beneath the solid warmth of Jacques's trembling little form. She'd rather die than let Dalton see the effect he had on her, especially after his dig about her work ethic. Or lack thereof.

She really couldn't stand that smug look in his eye, but what she despised even more was the fact that he'd been right. She'd never worked a day in her life. Not technically. Of course she'd always considered being royal a job in and of itself. But being here in New York and seeing how many people it took to keep Drake Diamonds running day in and day out, made her painfully aware of how easy she had it, her dreaded arranged marriage notwithstanding.

Like it or not, Dalton had been right about her to some extent. She'd come to New York for a taste of real life, but holing up in a workaholic diamond heir's luxury apartment wasn't any more real than life in a palace.

It feels real, though. At the moment, nothing in the world felt as real as the forbidden heat of Dalton's palm in the small of her back as he escorted her down the hall. A tremble coursed through her, and for some ridiculous reason she felt like crying as the Engagements showroom came into view.

"Are you all right?" he asked, much to her horror.

Get it together, Aurélie. She refused to break down in front of Dalton Drake. She'd have nine uninterrupted hours to cry all she wanted on her flight back to Delamotte.

"I'm perfectly fine," she said as Jacques licked a tear from her cheek.

Dalton stared at her for a beat, and a dangerous-looking knot formed in his jaw. He looked like he could grind coal into diamonds with his teeth. Tears made him angry? It figured, seeing as he seemed allergic to the full scale of human emotions.

"You're fine. Clearly," he muttered and jabbed at the elevator's down button.

The elevator attendant, who felt almost like a friend by now, was nowhere to be seen. He must have gone home for the day. Aurélie stared straight ahead as the doors slid closed, despite the array of sparkling diamond engagement rings assaulting her vision. She didn't dare venture another glance at Dalton while they were trapped together in a small, enclosed space. Not after what she'd done the last time they were in a similar situation.

"Is it true that Gaston Drake invented the concept of

the engagement ring?" she asked, purely for something to say to pierce the sultry silence.

She wasn't even sure where she'd picked up the bit of trivia about Dalton's great-great-great-great-great-grandfather. Probably from one of the brochures she'd had time to all but memorize while Dalton left her unattended in his office.

"Been reading up on the company, have you?" His voice carried a note of surprise.

"I *can* read, you know. I have a master's degree from the Sorbonne." Granted, she'd completed most of her coursework long-distance. But Dalton didn't need to know that. "Does that surprise you, Mr. Drake?"

She couldn't help herself, and glanced up at him for the briefest second. Big mistake. Huge.

Instead of finding a superior glint in his eye, as she'd come to expect, he was appraising her with a penetrating stare. As if he could see every part of her, inside and out, and despite his penchant for mocking her, he liked what he saw.

The corner of his lips curved into a half grin. "You have a habit of surprising me on a daily basis, Princess."

Aurélie blinked, and despite every effort to maintain respectable, chaste eye contact, her gaze dropped straight to his mouth.

It was happening again. She was thinking about kissing him. She was thinking about his hands in her hair and the cold fury of his lips and the delicious ache that was beginning to stir low in her belly. Just under five minutes in the man's presence was all it had taken.

They didn't even like each other. What on earth was wrong with her?

Thank God for the squirming puppy in her arms. He

was the only thing keeping her from making a complete and utter fool of herself. Again.

Somewhere amid the fog of arousal, she was vaguely aware of a bell ringing and a whooshing sound, followed by Dalton's voice saying her name.

"Hmm?" she heard herself say.

"We're here. The ground floor." He stood beside her, holding the elevator door open, eyeing her with concern. She'd been so lost in illicit thought that she hadn't even noticed the elevator had come to a stop. "Are you quite sure you're all right?"

No. Not one bit. "Yes, of course."

She brushed past him, out of the elevator and into the gleaming lobby. She was immediately taken aback by the unexpected serenity of the showroom. There wasn't a soul in sight, not even a salesperson. As soon as she set foot on the marble foyer floor, the overhead lights flickered and dimmed.

The store was closing? Already?

She still hadn't uttered a word to Dalton about leaving. Nor had she even seen her egg since the day she'd arrived.

"You forgot your coat." Dalton paused in front of the revolving door and frowned down at her bare arms.

She sighed. Time was running out. There was no way she was going to go all the way back to the kitchen for her coat, especially if it meant another ride up and down the elevator with Dalton, filled with sexual tension.

She plopped Jacques on the floor, wrapped his leash around her wrist and crossed her arms. "I'll be fine like this. We'll hurry."

Thankfully, Dalton didn't look any more inclined than

she was to get back into the elevator. He glanced at his watch and his frown deepened.

"Don't be ridiculous." Dalton slipped out of his overcoat and placed it around her shoulders. "Here."

Despite the stormy disapproval in his gray gaze, or maybe because of it, an undeniable thrill coursed through Aurélie at the intimacy of the gesture. She turned her head as she obediently slid her arms into the sleeves of his coat, because it was just too much, this sudden closeness. His coat was impossibly soft— cashmere, obviously—and warm from the heat of his body. Dalton's face was right there, just inches away from hers as he buttoned her up, and all at once she was enveloped in him. His woodsy clean scent. His sultry warmth. All of him.

Aurélie's heart thundered against her ribs, and she prayed he couldn't hear it. She didn't trust herself to look at him, so she focused instead on the dazzling array of jewels behind him, sparkling and shimmering in their illuminated display cases. Treasures in the dark.

"There," Dalton muttered with a trace of huskiness in his voice that seemed to scrape Aurélie's insides.

She had to say something. If she didn't do it now, she might never go through with it.

The revolving doors were flanked on either side by two large banners advertising the upcoming exhibit of the Marchand imperial eggs. The first and oldest egg of the collection, known as the jeweled hen egg, was pictured on a pristine white background. This particular egg stood out from the rest as the simplest in design. On the surface, it looked almost like an actual egg. But in reality, it had been crafted from solid gold and coated in creamy white enamel. Upon close inspection, a barely discernible gold line was visible along the egg's center, where its two halves were joined. Once the hidden fitting was opened, a round gold yolk could be found nestled inside. And inside the yolk, a diamond-encrusted platinum crown. A precious, priceless secret.

Aurélie stared at the image of her family heirloom looming larger than life over Dalton's shoulder. *So many secrets.*

She was thoroughly sick of all of them.

"There's something I need to tell you," she heard herself say.

Dalton arched a single eyebrow. "So you said."

She swallowed. The words were gathering in her throat. She could taste their ripeness on the tip of her tongue and still she wasn't quite sure what form they would take.

You're right about me. I'm every bit as silly and irresponsible as you suspect.

I'm engaged to be married.

I'm leaving.

"I..." she started, but a sharp bark pierced the loaded silence. Then another, followed by a wholly impatient canine growl.

Aurélie looked down at Jacques, who'd stretched himself into a downward dog position that would have made even the most die-hard yogi green with envy. He woofed again and wagged his stump of a tail.

"Hold that thought," Dalton said. "I've already cleaned up after your little monster enough times today."

He strode toward the revolving door with Jacques nipping at his heels, and Aurélie had no choice but to follow. They made their way down the block to Central Park and back without uttering another word. There was something about the gently falling snow and the quiet city streets awash with white that forbade conversation.

A chill coursed through her, and she slipped her hands in the pockets of Dalton's overcoat. The fingertips of her right hand made contact with something buried in the silk pocket lining. Something small. Round. Familiar.

She knew without even looking at it that the object in her hand was one of her mother's pearls. A broken reminder of their kiss.

Aurélie was painfully aware of each passing second. Time seemed to be moving far more quickly than usual, in a twilight violet-hued blur. She couldn't help but wonder if Dalton felt it, too, especially when the echo of his footsteps on the bluestone slate sidewalk seemed to grow further and further apart.

They could walk as slowly as they wanted, but they'd never be able to stop time. Midnight was approaching, and if she didn't ask for her egg back now—right now— it would be too late. Even if she wanted to stay, she couldn't.

She glanced up at the amethyst sky and the billowing snow, like something out of a fairy tale, and told herself to remember this. Remember the magic of the bustling city. Remember what it felt like to be wrapped in borrowed cashmere with frost in her hair. Remember the music falling down from the stars.

Music?

She blinked. "Do you hear that?" she whispered.

"Hear what?" Dalton paused alongside her.

"Music." Aurélie slowed to a stop, and Jacques plopped into a lopsided sitting position at her feet. "Listen."

She couldn't quite grab hold of it, and for a split second she thought she must have only imagined the plaintive sounds of a violin floating above the distant blare of horns and the thrum of city's heartbeat center. But then she closed her eyes and when she did, she found it again.

"Do you hear it? Vivaldi." Her eyelashes fluttered open, and beyond the puff of her breath in the frosty air, she saw Dalton watching her with an intensity that made her cheeks go warm. She swallowed. "Where do you think it's coming from?"

He looked at her for a moment that seemed to stretch far too long, then he took her hand. "I'll show you."

She started to protest before she realized they were covering familiar territory, treading the now-familiar path back toward Drake Diamonds. They passed the entrance to the Plaza Hotel with its grand white pillars and crimson steps, and as they walked beneath the ghostly glow of gas lamplights, the music grew louder and louder. It swelled to a crescendo just as the violinist came into view.

He was situated right beside the entrance to Drake Diamonds with a tip bucket at his feet. Eyes closed, hands covered with fingerless mitts, he moved his bow furiously over the instrument. He was just a street musician, but Aurélie had never seen a violinist play with such passion, not even at Delamotte's royal symphony. He was so lost in his music that a lump formed in Aurélie's throat as she stood watching him, grinning from ear to ear.

For a perfect, precious moment, she forgot she was supposed to be saying goodbye. She forgot she shouldn't be standing in the dark, holding Dalton's hand. She forgot that when she looked up at him, she'd find the sculpted planes of his face so beautiful that she'd go breathless. He reminded her of all those diamonds glittering in their lonely display cases in the dark. Hard. Exquisite. Forever beyond her reach.

"It's lovely, isn't it?" she breathed.

At the sound of her voice, the music abruptly stopped.

"I'm sorry, Mr. Drake." The violinist bent to return his instrument to its case.

Clearly he'd been forewarned against occupying the precious sidewalk space in front of Drake Diamonds. As if Dalton owned the entire walkway where they were standing.

He probably does.

"Don't stop, it's okay. Please continue." Without tearing his gaze from Aurélie, Dalton reached into his suit pocket for his wallet, pulled out a thick wad of bills and tossed them in the musician's tip bucket. He angled his head toward her. "Anything in particular you'd like to hear, Princess?"

Princess. His voice didn't have the bite to it that she'd grown accustomed to. On the contrary, he said the word almost as if it were an endearment.

Tell him. Just say it—I'm leaving.

Maybe she could have if his gaze hadn't gone tender and if he'd looked less like a tragic literary hero all of a sudden rather than what he was—a ruthless, self-contained diamond heir. Instead, she heard herself say, "How about some Gershwin?"

His handsome face split into a rare, unguarded grin. "Gershwin? How very New York of you." He shrugged and called out to the violinist. "You heard the lady. I don't suppose you know any Gershwin?"

The familiar, sweeping strains of "Rhapsody in Blue" filled the air, and Aurélie couldn't even bring herself to look at Dalton, much less utter a goodbye. So she focused intently on the violinist instead.

"He's quite good, isn't he?" Dalton said.

She nodded and pretended not to notice the overwhelming magic of the moment. "Perfect."

The song had always been a favorite of hers, but she'd never heard it like this before. Not with the notes rising and floating over the city as snowflakes danced and spun in the glow of the streetlights. It was at once altogether beautiful yet hauntingly sad.

She turned toward Dalton. He had that look about him again, a fleeting tragic edge that drew her fingertips to her throat in search of her mother's pearls even though she knew they were no longer there.

"About earlier…in the tenth floor showroom," he said, his gaze searching.

The tenth floor showroom. Engagements. So he'd noticed her unease at being surrounded by all those wedding rings? Of course he had.

He smiled, but it didn't quite reach his eyes. "For what it's worth, Engagements isn't my favorite department, either."

She wasn't sure what she'd expected him to say, but it certainly hadn't been that. *"Non?"*

He shook his head. "I despise it, actually."

They had something in common after all. She couldn't help but wonder why he felt that way. *Despise* was an awfully strong word. But she didn't dare ask, lest he reciprocate with questions of his own.

She offered only a wry smile. "Not the marrying type?"

He didn't respond, just stared straight ahead. Whatever tenderness she'd seen in his gaze earlier had evaporated, replaced by the cool indifference she'd come to know so well over the past few days.

She rolled her eyes. "Right. Why am I surprised when you're so clearly married to your work?"

"Something like that." The coldness in his voice made her wince, and he kept his gaze fixed on the musician. Then, as if the awkward exchange had never happened, he said, "Shall we dance?"

She let out a laugh. Surely he'd meant the offer as a joke. "Isn't there a spreadsheet somewhere that needs your attention?"

His eyes flashed in the darkness. "I'm dead serious. Dance with me."

He slid one arm around her waist and took her hand with the other. He pulled her close, so close that she could feel the full length of his body pressed against hers. A tight, hard wall of muscle. She wasn't at all prepared for such sudden closeness. The confidence with which he held her and the warmth of his fingertips on her wrist was disorienting, and before she knew what was happening, they were floating over the snowy sidewalk.

The world slowed to a stop. In a city of millions, it felt as if they were the only two people on earth. Aurélie was scarcely aware of the violinist's presence, nor of Jacques's leash winding itself slowly around their legs. Tears gathered in her eyes. She had to stop herself from burying her face in his chest and pressing her lips to the side of his neck.

She wanted to cry, because how could she possibly walk away now, when this would undoubtedly be the most romantic moment of her life?

"You've gone awfully quiet all of sudden," he whispered, and his voice rumbled through her like distant thunder.

It was strange the things people remembered when they found themselves at an impasse. Aurélie's mind should have been on the pink enamel egg coated in seed pearls that was sitting inside the Drake Diamonds vault. She should have been trying to figure out a way to get herself back home. Instead, she suddenly remembered something Artem had said earlier in the kitchen.

Don't you have something you need to discuss with Aurélie, Dalton?

She'd been so nervous about announcing her early departure that she'd forgotten the way Dalton's jaw had hardened in response to Artem's question. She glanced up at him now. "Wasn't there something you wanted to tell me?"

He fixed his gaze with hers, and Aurélie saw something new in his eyes. A fleeting hesitancy. Above them, the darkness of the night sky felt heavy, swollen with so many words left unspoken between them. Everything they wouldn't, couldn't, say.

"It can wait," he said.

She nodded, and somehow she knew there would be no goodbyes. Not now. Not tonight.

Their legs became too entangled in the dog leash to keep dancing, so they slowed to a stop until they were standing still in one another's arms. The music may have gone quiet. Aurélie wasn't even sure. She'd slipped into a hazy, dreamlike state, drunk on music and sensation.

Dalton reached, wove his fingers through hers and brushed his lips against the back of her hand. "Let's go home."

Aurélie took a deep breath. If she didn't leave for the

airport right now, she'd miss her flight. She'd never get to Paris in time to catch a connection to Delamotte. She'd miss her appointment with Lord Clement.

The palace would undoubtedly come looking for her, and there would be no turning back. Not this time.

One more day. Just one more day.

Dalton released her hand and bent to untangle Jacques's leash. He walked a few steps in the direction of his apartment building with the little bulldog trotting alongside him, then turned and stopped. Waited. "Are you coming, Princess?"

"Oui. Une seconde." She reached into the pocket of Dalton's coat for the lonely gold pearl, held it tightly in her closed fist then dropped it in the violinist's tip bucket, where it swirled to an iridescent stop in the moonlight.

No turning back.

Chapter Nine

This is a mistake.

Dalton was fully aware of what would happen when he made the fatal choice to take Aurélie back to the apartment instead of to the airport. He knew what he was doing was wrong. Reckless. Probably even downright dangerous.

He'd been so prepared to tell her it would be best if she went back home. He'd waited all day for her to show up so he could break the news to her in person. Her little holiday was over. He was a busy man. He didn't have time to babysit a princess. Especially a princess who wore her heart on her sleeve the way that Aurélie did.

She wasn't anything like the other women who'd been in Dalton's life. More specifically, the women who'd been in his bed. If the problem had been as simple as sex, and sex alone, he would have broken down and succumbed to temptation by now.

But he had the distinct feeling that sex with Aurélie would be anything but simple. She got emotional over street musicians and homeless puppies and hot dogs.

To Dalton's complete and utter astonishment, he found it charming. Sexy. Altogether irresistible, if he was being honest.

Which was precisely the problem. Aurélie wasn't a woman he could just sleep with and then move on. She'd only been in his life for a few days, and in that small span of time, she'd thrown his entire existence into an uproar. She was sentimental to her core. She was also a runaway royal princess.

But he couldn't seem to resist taking her hand and leading her home. He had to stop himself from kissing her on the grand steps of the library under the watchful gaze of the stone lions, their manes laden with snow. Patience and Fortitude. Dalton had neither at the moment. But he knew if he kissed her then, beneath the moon and the stars and the ethereal lamplight glow, he'd be unable to stop.

At his building, the doorman nodded a greeting. Dalton must have said something in return, but he couldn't imagine what. He couldn't hear a thing over the roar of blood in his ears and the annoying howl of his conscience.

This is a mistake.

Dalton no longer believed in mistakes. Not tonight. Not now, when Aurélie was looking at him with eyes full of bejeweled longing. Not when it seemed as if the walls of the cool marble lobby hummed with desire and the wild percussion of their hearts.

He didn't wait for the elevator to deposit them on the penthouse floor. Couldn't. The doors slid closed with a sultry whisper, and he held Aurélie's glittering gaze until he was sure—absolutely certain—that she wanted this as badly as he did.

Then he moved toward her with a growl—a deep, primitive sound he'd never heard himself make before—and crushed his mouth to hers.

Aurélie melted into him with a slow, drawn-out inhale and slid the palms of her hands languidly up his chest. He closed his eyes and lost himself in the warm wonderland of her mouth and the quickening flutter of her breath as the kiss grew deeper.

More demanding.

The ground beneath them stirred as the elevator lifted them closer to the stars, farther and farther from the real world down below. Aurélie's delicate form felt weightless, feather-light in his arms, and he was hit with a momentary panic at the thought that she might float away.

He leaned closer, closer, until he'd pressed her against the elevator wall. His hands moved to her slender wrists and circled them loosely like bracelets. Her body softened. The dog's leash slipped from her fingers and fell to the floor. She whispered his name, and the aching hunger in her voice was so raw, so sweetly vulnerable, that it nearly brought him to his knees.

Everything went white hot. Like a diamond burning away to smoke.

Dalton was harder than he'd ever been in his life. He was seconds away from sliding his hand under her dress, up the luxurious length of her thigh, and stroking his way inside her with his fingers.

He wanted to make her come. He wanted to watch her go someplace she'd never been, knowing he was the one who'd taken her there. The only one.

He was fairly certain she was a virgin, which only

multiplied the severity of the mistake he was about to make. She was a princess, and seemed to have lived a sheltered existence. She had an air of innocent charm about her. He could still think coherently enough for that fact to register somewhere in his consciousness. But he no longer gave a damn about right and wrong. About who either of them were.

If she was a virgin, though, he needed to slow down. Be gentle. And he certainly shouldn't be on the verge of undressing her in an elevator. She deserved better than this.

"Aurélie," he groaned, pulling back to rest his forehead against hers and twirl a lock of her spun-gold hair around his fingertip.

He could see her pulse hammering in her throat, and he wanted to kiss it. To press his mouth, wet and wanting, against the life teeming beneath her porcelain skin.

"Please," she pleaded, just as she'd done in the car on the afternoon she'd kissed him, and Dalton knew he was done for.

Mistake or not, he couldn't let her down again. Perhaps a better man could, a more honorable man. But Dalton had never felt less honorable in his life.

For each and every one of his thirty-three years, he'd done exactly what was expected of him. Where had it gotten him? The empty place he currently occupied—nowhere. Nothing was as it should be.

He'd had enough. Enough of duty. Enough of restraint. Enough of denying himself what he wanted. It had been a long, long time since he'd wanted anything. Anyone. So many lost years.

And now he wanted Aurélie.

At last he remembered what it was like to want and

need and ache. But the way he felt when he looked at her, when he touched her, wasn't anything like a memory. It was better. It was intoxicating.

The elevator came to a stop. Finally. Dalton took Aurélie's hand and led her inside the apartment. Somehow, he kept his wits about him long enough to get the dog settled in his spacious laundry room with a rawhide chew and a stuffed toy that would no doubt be disemboweled by morning. Which was perfectly fine with Dalton, so long as the little troublemaker was content.

He found Aurélie waiting for him in the darkened living room. The sight of her standing there with her ruby-red lips slightly parted and swollen from his kisses, eyes bright, made him want to tell her all kinds of truths. He had to clench his jaw to keep them from spilling out.

Her back was to the window, where snow beat against the glass in a dizzying fury. The night was steeped in winter white, but Dalton had gone summer warm.

"Let me look at you," he said as he approached. "I want to see you."

Without a trace of shyness, she reached for the hem of her dress and slipped it over her head. If she was nervous, she didn't let it show. On the contrary, her knowing smile gave him the impression that she was well aware of the effect she had on him.

She knew, and she quite enjoyed it.

Her dress landed on the floor in a polka-dot whisper. With her generous waves of hair tumbling over one moonstone shoulder, she lifted her bowed head and raised her gaze to his.

Dalton had to pause for a moment and collect himself. It hurt to swallow. It hurt to breathe. Every cell in his body screamed in agony, waiting and wanting to touch her.

He stared at her too hard and too long—at the willowy length of her legs, the captivating dip between her collarbones, the generous swell of her breasts covered in pale pink lace, a prelude to her softness.

The space between them shimmered with promise.

Everything about her was heavenly. Dalton would have loved to drape her bare body in ropes of pearls, to adorn her glorious curves with the precious treasures of the South Sea. Aurélie deserved such adoration. She deserved everything.

What was it about this woman, this near stranger who filled him with such decadent thoughts and so thoroughly shattered his reserve?

She's not just a woman. She's a princess.

She was royalty. And for tonight, she was his.

Aurélie had been waiting for this moment for what felt like an eternity.

Days ago, if she'd known she would be standing in Dalton Drake's living room in nothing but her bra and panties while he, fully clothed, looked his fill, she wouldn't have believed it. The very idea would have made her blush.

She wasn't blushing now. It felt natural, right, predestined somehow, that she should be here at this exact place and time. A rare and precious moment that had somehow been lost. Forgotten. Waiting for Aurélie to step into it when time had reached its fulfillment.

Dalton's gaze was serious. Grave even, as his gray eyes glittered with intent. He wasn't just looking at her.

He was studying her, and she felt every hard stare as surely as if he'd reached out and touched her.

Why hadn't he touched her yet? How long was he going to stand there and watch her burn? The slow simmer that had begun the morning he'd first set his gaze on her from across the chaste expanse of his desk had become intolerable. Liquid heat pooled at her center, and fire skittered over skin in the wake of his gaze.

She needed his hands on her. His mouth. On her. Inside her. She thought she might die if he made her wait much longer, and she couldn't hide her desperation. Her pride had fallen away with the whisper of her dress dropping to the floor. She was too inflamed to feel any sense of embarrassment.

Eyes locked with his, she walked toward him. One purposeful step—that's all she remembered taking, because he moved toward her at the exact same time. And suddenly his hands were everywhere—in her hair, cupping her bottom, sliding beneath the wispy lace cups of her bra and skimming over her sensitive nipples with the softest of touches. Her body all but wept with relief.

He kissed her again, and this time his lips were deliberate. Knowing. She realized every other kiss had been nothing but a prelude. This time, he took her mouth, possessed it as if he were already buried deep inside her. She kissed him back, arching toward him without even realizing she'd moved.

Her arousal astounded her. Shocked her to her core. Aurélie Marchand, the dutiful princess, had vanished and been replaced by a stranger. A stranger whose body was crying out for relief. A stranger who did things like slip out of her bra, reach for Dalton's hands and place them on her bare breasts.

"So beautiful," he whispered.

She loved the way he touched her. The way his big, capable hands cradled her as if he were holding a bone china teacup. Graceful with purpose.

He lowered his mouth to her nipple and at the first touch of his warm, wet tongue, Aurélie's knees went weak. She fell against him, and he wrapped an arm around her waist, holding her in place as he devoured her.

His hands slipped inside her panties, pushing them down until she was completely naked. She wanted him to undress, too, so she could see him, touch him, feel the hard ripple of his muscles beneath her fingertips. But as her hands sought the lapels of his suit jacket, one of Dalton's hands slid between her thighs.

She opened for him, and he stared down at her without breaking his gaze as he slipped a finger inside.

Oh my God.

"Aurélie, princess, have you ever been with a man before?"

She bit her lip to keep the truth from spilling out. She could never lie to him, not when those devastating eyes of his saw straight through her the way that they did. But she was afraid to tell him the truth, to admit there'd never been another.

She wanted him to be her first. She needed this more than Dalton ever could, or ever would, know. Right now a plane was bound for Delamotte, and her seat was empty. But the palace was waiting, and it wouldn't wait forever. She would never have a chance like this again.

Still, she was terrified to actually go through with it. Because somewhere beneath her quivering need, the truth shined bright. A fire opal of awareness.

This was more than just physical. She cared for Dalton. She might even be in love with him.

No. No, I'm not. I do not *love him. I can't.*

She squeezed her eyes shut tight, but it was too late. The truth had settled itself in her bones, in the liquid embers flowing through her veins. She wasn't just giving her body to Dalton. She was giving him her soul, her heart, her everything. And God help her, she had no idea how she was going to walk away and take it all back.

Dalton's hand grew still, and his fingers stopped the delicious thing they were doing between her legs. She could feel him waiting, willing her to answer him. "Tell me, princess. I need to know."

There's never been anyone else. Only you. Always you.

"No." She reached between them and slid her hand over his, holding it in place as she ground against him, crushing her breasts against his chest until he released an agonizing moan. What had come over her? *Don't stop. Please don't stop. Please.* "I haven't, but..."

"Shh. It's okay." His voice was a tortured whisper, his breath hot against the curve of her neck. "We'll go slow."

She nodded, unable to form words. Unable to do anything but feel. Feel and sigh her surrender.

She was a virgin, but she wasn't completely naïve. She knew what went on between a man and a woman.

She'd thought she did, anyway.

She realized now that she knew nothing. How could she have possibly anticipated how overwhelming this would be? How utterly sublime?

Because this is special. This is love.

"No."

Dalton tilted his head. "No?"

Had she actually said that out loud? She swallowed and with trembling fingertips, unfastened the Windsor knot in his Drake-blue tie. "I don't want it slow. I want you inside me. Now."

In a single, unhesitating movement, he tossed the tie aside and shed his jacket. The desire in his eyes hardened, grew sharp, until it was a blazing, furious thing. Aurélie's breath caught in her throat, and the first traces of nerves fluttered low in her belly.

This was the end, the dying embers of the moment in between. They were going someplace else now. Someplace new. A place with no means of return. He swept an arm beneath her legs, scooped her against his chest and carried her there.

Behind a lacy veil of snow, moonlight streamed in through the bedroom windows. Dalton deposited her in the center of his massive bed, and before her eyes were fully adjusted to the cool blue shadows of the semidarkness, he'd pulled his shirt over his head and unfastened his belt.

She rose to her knees, reaching for him. She was afraid—not of what was about to happen, but about how it would end.

He was so beautiful. Beautiful and male and daunting in his intensity. She craved this intimacy far more than she feared its consequences, what it would do to her when the time had come to leave. She lifted her mouth to his, hungry and desperate, and he groaned into it as her hand slid inside his trousers, finding his steely length.

He was far bigger than she'd imagined. Big and diamond hard. She didn't know how in the world she could accommodate his size, couldn't even fathom how it would work, but she didn't care.

His breath had gone ragged, his eyelids heavy, and it thrilled her to know she could make him feel this way. That just by touching him the right way, she could make him let go of even a little bit of his steadfast control.

"Darling," he whispered, pushing her back on the bed, covering her body with his.

At last they were skin to skin, limbs intertwined, hands exploring. The weight of him on top of her was exquisite, and his erection pressed hot and wanting between her legs. Then he was pushing inside, past the bittersweet whisper of pain, and she was rising up to meet him. Wanting, wanting, wanting, until at long last, she was full.

He paused, giving her time to adjust, and finally he began to move. Thrusting, gently at first, with slow, measured strokes.

"More," she heard herself say, and she wrapped her legs around him, pulling him closer. And closer still. She wanted it all. Everything he could give. Even the parts of him he wouldn't.

He groaned, pumped faster, and something hot and wild gathered at Aurélie's center. Stars glittered behind her eyes, and she rested a palm on Dalton's chest, searching for something solid. Steady. A pulse to keep her grounded.

But she was too far gone, lost to sensation. She could only breathe and give herself up to the wondrous free fall of the climax bearing down on her. Beneath her fingertips, Dalton's heart pounded a constant beat.

Mine.

Mine.

Mine.

A rebellious tear slid down Aurélie's cheek. The snow spun its gentle dance and Dalton gazed down at her with a look so tender that she was certain she felt her heart rip in two even as she found her shuddering, shimmering release.

Chapter Ten

It couldn't happen again. Of that, Aurélie was absolutely certain.

She was certain of it in the middle of the night when she found herself tangled in the bed sheets with Dalton's head between her thighs. She was certain of it when she cried his name again and again to the diamond-studded sky. And she was *especially* certain of it when she woke in the morning reaching for him, tears welling in her eyes.

He wasn't there. The bed was still warm where he'd been. His heady, masculine scent still clung to his pillow. Aurélie closed her eyes, inhaled and lifted her arms over her head, stretching languidly. A cat who'd gotten the cream.

But the cat had no business tasting the cream. The cream was off-limits. And now that the cat had indulged, she wouldn't be satisfied with just a bland drop of milk. Ever.

Aurélie's eyes flew open, and she sat up, panicked. She began to tremble deep inside, as if her bones were trying to shake off the mistake she'd just made.

What had she done?

This was bad. She'd given herself to Dalton in every possible way. She'd meant to offer him her body, but somewhere along the way, she'd accidently given him her heart. And now she was rolling around in his bed like she belonged there when she clearly did not.

From the spacious master bath, she could hear the shower running. The rich scent of espresso hung in the air. She leaped out of the bed, determined not to let Dalton find her here when he returned. *If* he returned.

Would he come looking for her before he left for work? Would he cradle her face and claim her mouth as he'd done the night before? Over and over again, until her lips felt bruised. Taken.

A ribbon of liquid longing wound its way through her at the mere thought of his wicked mouth, his capable hands. Of his lean, hard muscles and the way her head fit perfectly in the space between his neck and shoulder.

Her body was deliciously sore from their lovemaking. It was almost as if she could still feel him inside her. And that phantom sensation made her want him all over again. Just thinking about it made her go all tingly inside.

Her heart gave a little lurch.

What was she going to do?

She couldn't bear to leave. Not now. But the longer she waited, the harder it would become. She should have never slow-danced with Dalton. She should have never made love with him. Because that was what it had been. Not sex—making love. At least that was what it had been for her. She wholeheartedly doubted Dalton felt the same way.

Even if he did, what difference would it make?

She glanced down at her bare ring finger and tried to imagine what it would look like adorned with a diamond engagement ring. Her vision grew blurry behind a veil of tears and she clenched her fist until nails dug into her palm.

Breathe. Just breathe.

Her lungs burned, and her throat felt scratchy. She climbed out of bed, looked around and found her lingerie in a lacy, decadent trail leading to the living room. The pretty new polka dot dress was pooled on the floor by the window. Scattered shoes, coats and Dalton's discarded tie painted such a vivid picture of what had gone on the night before that a lump formed in her throat as she gathered them all up.

She could straighten as much as she wanted. She could put the room back together again, even toss the clothes in the garbage, but it wouldn't change anything. There was no way to undo what she'd done. She couldn't take it back.

Even if she could, she wouldn't. Not in a million years.

Which was precisely why it wouldn't, *couldn't*, happen again.

Fresh from a cold shower, yet still inexplicably aroused beyond all reason, Dalton strolled naked toward the bedroom.

His appetite for Aurélie was insatiable. He couldn't quite understand it. Didn't want to. He'd think about it later. Much later, after he'd taken her to bed once more.

Just one more time.

Then he'd end things before they got too complicated.

Right. They'd passed *complicated* ages ago. He thought of the pink enameled egg. Their bargain. Artem's warning.

In all seriousness, have you thought about what you're going to do when they realize she's missing? Surely someone will notice.

How had he allowed things to get so far out of hand?

He needed to end it. Now. For Aurélie's sake as much as for the sake of Drake Diamonds. Because she didn't know what Dalton knew all too well—leaving New York and returning to Delamotte was the best possible thing she could do. A blessing, really. If she stayed, he'd hurt her. He didn't want to, but he would.

He'd done it before, and he couldn't risk doing it again. Not to Aurélie.

The mere thought of it caused a familiar darkness to gather inside him. Like a terrible smoke. A black, suffocating fog that threatened to swallow him up.

With each step Dalton took to the bedroom, though, it lifted. Because when he was with Aurélie, when he was buried deep inside her, he could almost forget the things he'd done. The mistakes he'd made.

He could breathe again.

Almost.

The darkness descended again when he found his bed empty. Not just empty, but completely made.

Dalton glowered at the crisp white duvet, pulled so neatly over the king-size mattress that there wasn't a wrinkle in sight. His gaze drifted toward the headboard. He couldn't believe what he was seeing. Where had Aurélie learned the art of hospital corners? He would have bet money she'd never even made a bed before. He probably would have found such a surprise amusing if it hadn't rubbed him so entirely the wrong way.

He was profoundly irritated, and the very fact that he felt this way irritated him further. Because it forced him to admit the truth he'd been trying so hard to avoid—his control was beginning to slip.

The cold shower...the coffee...neither had done a damn thing to snap him back into reality. Sunlight streamed through the bedroom windows. At his feet, the city was waking up beneath a fresh blanket of snow. Morning sparkled like an upturned sugar bowl.

But Dalton wasn't ready. Not even close. He was still lost in the opulent darkness of the night before.

This wasn't as he'd planned. He'd allowed himself one night, and one night only. One night to get Aurélie out of his system so he could get back to business.

Of course the fact that she'd indeed been a virgin gave him pause. He should have stopped things the moment she'd confirmed his suspicions in that regard. He couldn't have, though. Not if his life had depended on it.

What had he done?

An aching tightness formed in his chest. He took a deep breath, but the feeling didn't go away. It lingered, much like the memory of Aurélie's touch, her taste. The sweetness of her voice in his ear.

I don't want it slow. I want you inside me. Now.

He stared down at the neatly made bed, wondering what it meant. Nothing probably. He was overthinking things, as he'd always been prone to do.

It was getting late, anyway. The driver was scheduled to pick them up in less than half an hour. Dalton dressed quickly, then strode into the living room in search of Aurélie. He found her perched on one of his kitchen barstools reading yesterday's *New York Times* with Jacques sitting regally in her lap. The fact that she was fully dressed wasn't lost on him. He hadn't realized how badly he'd hoped to find her in a state of undress until now. Seeing her again, now that he'd been inside her, now that he knew what it was like to have those lithe legs wrapped around him, was like getting punched hard in the solar plexus. He swayed a little and gripped the edge of the countertop before he lost his head and gave in to the impulse to kiss her.

He thought of his neatly made bed and its damned hospital corners, but still his gaze found its way to Aurélie's mouth. Her pillowy lips were darker than usual, as red as the deep crimson center of a ruby. Swollen from his lavish attention.

His cock throbbed to life. Again. "Good morning," he said coolly.

"Good morning," she said, barely looking up from the newspaper.

The dog, on the other hand, stared straight at him. Dalton could have sworn he saw a trace of mockery in the French bulldog's big round eyes.

Dalton suppressed a sigh.

Jealous of the damned dog? Yet again? Pathetic.

He was losing it. But he'd be damned if he was going to stand there and pretend nothing had happened between them.

"Shall we talk about last night?" He crossed his arms, leaned against the counter and waited.

Jacques sighed and dropped his chin on the countertop as if the sheer weight of his head was more than he could handle. Which wouldn't have surprised Dalton in the least.

Aurélie rested one of her elegant hands between the dog's ears. There was a telltale tremble in her fingertips.

She devoted too much care to folding her newspaper into a tidy square, took a beat too long to meet his gaze. "If you'd like."

She was pretending.

Dalton wasn't sure why, but she obviously wanted to act like nothing had changed. When in fact everything had.

"I enjoyed it." *Don't touch her. Do not.* He shoved his hands in his trouser pockets. "Very much."

He could hear the catch in her breath, could see the pink flush rise to her cheeks.

She kept up her charade, clearing her throat. "As did I, but…"

He lifted his brows. "But?" he repeated, sounding harsher than he intended.

The dog rolled its eyes, or maybe that was just Dalton's imagination.

Aurélie lifted her chin. "But I don't think it should happen again."

He looked at her, long and hard, as the darkness gathered in him again. Thick and suffocating. And for the first time, he realized it had a name. Regret.

"I understand." But he didn't understand. Not at all.

He had no business feeling as frustrated as he did. This was for the best. It was precisely what he'd wanted, wasn't it?

Yes. Yes, it is.

He was far from relieved, however. On the contrary, he was furious.

Aurélie's gaze flitted to the digital clock display on the microwave. "I suppose you're off to work now."

He would have liked nothing more than to escape to the quiet solitude of his office on the tenth floor of Drake Diamonds. But today of all days, he couldn't.

Perfect. Just perfect.

He shook his head. "No, actually."

Aurélie blinked. "No?"

"No." Dalton's cell phone buzzed with an incoming text message. He glanced down at it and cleared the display. "In fact, that's our ride."

"*Our* ride," she repeated with a telltale wobble in her voice.

Dalton nodded, stalked past her and reached for his jacket in the coat closet. He was half tempted to leave her behind. But something told him if he walked out the door, she might not be here when he returned.

Sure enough, as he pulled his Burberry wool coat from its hanger, he spotted a suitcase tucked away at the back of the closet. *His* suitcase, he noted wryly.

He looked pointedly at the bag and then at Aurélie, waiting for her to say something. If she wanted to go, he certainly wouldn't stop her.

That's right. Run away, Aurélie. Run away from me, just like you ran from whatever it is you're trying to escape in Delamotte.

He didn't know why he hadn't seen it coming. Of course she wouldn't stick around to honor their agreement.

Wasn't it just yesterday you wanted to send her away?

Dalton's jaw hardened. His hand twitched. He should pick up the suitcase and hand it to her. Along with a plane ticket.

He wasn't sure why he didn't.

If she left, he'd have the Marchand eggs to contend with. Articles about the exhibit were in every newspaper in New York. Banners were up in every showroom in the store. The Marchand eggs could be returned after the exhibit, as planned.

But what of the secret egg? What of their bargain?

A day ago he'd been prepared to let it go, to forget he'd ever set eyes on Aurélie and her glittering treasure. Now he refused to make that concession. Not when it wasn't his call, his choice. He controlled what went on at Drake Diamonds, not an impulsive princess who'd never worked a day in her life.

Aurélie's gaze flitted anywhere and everywhere *except* at the suitcase. She swallowed, and her hand fluttered to her throat.

Dalton did his best to ignore the flash of heat that rioted through him at the memory of his mouth upon her neck, the wild beat of her pulse beneath his lips.

"Where are we off to, then?" she asked, like they were a couple about to leave on holiday. Like the suitcase meant something that had no basis in reality.

Dalton shut the closet door. Out of sight, out of mind.

"We're going to the Hamptons."

Chapter Eleven

If Aurélie wasn't mistaken, Artem did a double take when she entered the Winter Hamptons Equestrian Classic's massive white tent on Dalton's arm.

"Aurélie, what a surprise." Charming as ever, Artem smiled. Astonishment aside, he seemed genuinely happy to see her. "How nice of you to join our family gathering. Dalton neglected to tell us you were coming along."

"Thank you so much for having me." The words left a bittersweet taste in her mouth.

Her voice felt raw, rusty. Probably because she and Dalton had only exchanged a handful of words during the tense ride to the Hamptons from the City. She'd sat beside him in the backseat of the town car while he pounded away on his laptop, and she felt it had been the longest three hours of her life.

She'd been so relieved when they'd pulled up to the

show grounds. She couldn't breathe with Dalton so close, not when every cell in her body was mourning the loss of his touch. She'd needed air. She'd needed space.

What she most definitely did *not* need was to be treated like a card-carrying member of the Drake fold.

Ophelia threw her arms around Aurélie and gave her a tight squeeze. "I'm so glad you're here. Wait until you see Diana ride. She's amazing."

Tears gathered behind Aurélie's eyes. She hadn't realized Artem and Ophelia would be there. Of course they were, though. It was a family event.

What am I doing here?

"I can't wait," she said, pulling away from Ophelia's embrace, aware of Dalton's gaze on her. Too aware.

This was almost worse than the car ride.

She glanced around, trying to get her bearings. Being inside the heated tent was like stepping into another world. If a fine layer of snow flurries hadn't still dusted Dalton's imposing shoulders, Aurélie might have forgotten they'd just come in from the cold.

The ground was covered in rich red dirt, a striking contrast to the snow piled outside. A course had been arranged in the large oval in the center of the tent with sets of rails painted stripes of red and white, flanked on either side by lush greenery and bright white flowers. Magnolias. Their sultry perfume hung heavy in the air, an unexpected luxury in the dead of winter.

Riders in breeches and glossy black boots walked around the outskirts of the arena, weaving between waiters holding silver trays of champagne flutes. An enormous gray horse strutted by, with its mane tightly woven in a braid snaking down its thickly muscled neck, and hooves so shiny Aurélie could see her reflection in them.

So this is the Hamptons.

Aurélie had never seen anything quite like it. Not even in Delamotte.

"It's something, isn't it?" Artem said, turning his back on all the opulence. A look Aurélie couldn't quite decipher passed between him and Dalton. "Diana is an Olympic hopeful, but I'm guessing my brother probably told you all about it."

Actually, no. We're not exactly speaking at the moment.

She forced her lips into a smile. "I'd love to hear more."

Aurélie wasn't about to admit that the man she'd slept with the night before—the man she thought she might be in love with—hadn't shared a single personal thing about himself in the entire time she'd known him. She didn't even want to admit such a thing to herself.

Fortunately, she'd been a princess all her life. Faking a smile was one of the job requirements.

That quality should come in handy when you're married three months from now.

Her gaze strayed rebelliously to Dalton. It hurt to look at him, to see the anger in his stormy eyes. It hurt even worse when she realized it wasn't only anger looking back at her, but disappointment as well.

She couldn't blame him. Not this time.

"Here she is now." Artem waved at a petite young woman making her way toward them.

She wore immaculate white breeches, a midnight-blue fitted riding jacket and a pair of neat white gloves. An elegant black horse pranced alongside her at the end of a blue lead rope. Drake blue.

She was definitely the woman from the screensaver

on Dalton's laptop. Same rich auburn hair twisted into a tight chignon. Same perfectly proportioned figure. Same confident smile. Dalton's sister.

Aurélie turned toward Dalton.

He lifted a brow. "Yes?"

"Are you going to tell your sister who I am?" she whispered.

Dalton frowned and muttered under his breath, "No. The fewer people who know, the better. Artem and Ophelia are involved with the business, so it makes sense for them to know. Let's leave Diana out of it."

"Good. I agree." They agreed on something. Miracles never ceased. "How are you going to explain my presence?"

"I'll introduce you as my friend, Aurélie." His *friend.* He looked down at her, and she saw too much on his face then—the fury and the heat still simmering between them. "She won't have any idea who you are. I doubt she's picked up a tabloid in years. Diana's life revolves around horses twenty-four seven."

"I see. So you typically bring dates to her horse shows, then?" Her face went hot with the effort it took not to sound like a jealous mistress, even though that was precisely what she was at the moment.

Pull yourself together.

Dalton's gaze strayed to her lips and lingered there. Long enough for Aurélie to grow breathless before he looked away without answering her question.

Diana greeted Artem with a warm embrace, gave Ophelia's tiny baby bump a gentle pat, then turned her attention to Dalton.

"Hi there, big brother. Thanks for tearing yourself away from the office to come see me jump." She threw her arms around him, all the while glancing curiously at Aurélie.

"Diana, this is Aurélie." Dalton's arm slid around Aurélie's waist, and she was immediately too aware of his palm resting against the curve of her hip. She fought the overwhelming impulse to melt into him.

Pathetic.

Dalton, on the other hand, seemed perfectly at ease. Impassive even. But when he looked down at her, she saw a spark of triumph in his gaze. He knew. He *knew.* He was all too aware he could drive her mad with the simplest touch, and he intended to use it to his full advantage.

"Aurélie, this is my sister, Diana Drake." His hand moved lower, his fingertips sweeping ever so lightly against her bottom.

"I'm delighted to meet you, Diana." She extended a hand and did her best to ignore her thumping heart and the way her skin suddenly felt too tight, like it could barely contain the riot of sensations skittering through her.

She wanted to strangle him.

Right after she kissed him again.

"The pleasure is all mine, I assure you." Diana ignored Aurélie's outstretched hand and pulled her into an enthusiastic embrace instead. The horse stood beside her, perfectly still other than the flicking of its glossy black tail.

"Diana," Dalton said, his voice tinged with warning.

"Ignore him," Diana whispered in Aurélie's ear. "He's all bark and no bite, in case you haven't noticed. Besides, I've been waiting for this for a long time. I haven't met one of Dalton's girlfriends since…"

"Okay, that's enough." Dalton pried the two of them apart.

Artem and Ophelia stood by, watching with amused interest.

Since when? Since whom?

Aurélie glanced at the suddenly firm set of Dalton's jaw and the flat, humorless line of his mouth. He steadfastly refused to look at her. Maybe she was just imagining the tension in the lines around his eyes. Then again, maybe not.

"We should take our seats. Surely you have last-minute things to attend to," he said, sounding more detached and robotic than Aurélie had ever heard him before.

Nope. Definitely not imagining things.

"Actually, Diamond and I are just about ready." Diana rested a hand on the horse's broad back.

Diamond's hide twitched and he stamped one hoof in greeting. His mane was braided into a graceful plait, and he'd been brushed and groomed to such an extent that he looked like a darkly elegant mirror.

"Your horse's name is Diamond? That certainly seems appropriate," Aurélie said.

"He's perfect. In showjumping a rider is only as good as her horse." Diana grinned. "Dalton bought him for me, actually. He had Diamond shipped over for me all the way from Europe."

"Did he?" She didn't quite know what to make of this news. The man was full of surprises.

"We can discuss something else now." The mysterious man in question cleared his throat.

Diana shot Aurélie a wink. "Excellent. Aurélie, why don't you tell me how you met my brother?"

Artem let out a hearty laugh.

"That wasn't what I had in mind," Dalton said flatly.

"Fine. Keep me guessing. I should probably get Diamond warmed up, anyway." Diana reached for Aurélie again and gave her another tight hug. "Thank you for coming. It was really a treat to meet you."

Aurélie wasn't accustomed to being embraced like that, especially since her mom had died. It caught her off guard.

And most of all, it made her realize what all she'd be leaving behind when she finally forced herself to leave New York. Not only Dalton, but a family. *His* family.

She'd miss seeing him like this.

She'd miss *him*.

"Good luck," she said, her breath growing shallower by the minute.

Then Diana was gone, and Artem was saying something. Aurélie wasn't sure what. A distant ringing had begun in her ears, and she had trouble hearing anything else.

What had she done?

She glanced at Dalton, at the planes of his handsome face and the dark layer of stubble on his jaw. But it was impossible for her to look at him without touching him, without wishing he would touch her in return. And she'd made it abundantly clear to him that was something she no longer wanted.

Now he would barely even look at her.

This is your doing. You did this.

She swallowed around the lump in her throat. How had she messed things up so badly? She'd been acting out of self-preservation, but suddenly she wanted to tell Dalton the truth. All of it.

She wanted to explain that she'd packed the suitcase the day before, not this morning. She wanted to confess why she'd left Delamotte. She wanted to tell him what she'd learned about her parents' marriage and about the fate that awaited her when she returned to the palace.

She wanted to tell him how she felt about him.

She wouldn't, of course. Couldn't. Not here. Not now. "I can't."

Dalton swiveled his gaze toward her. Finally.

Artem's brow furrowed. "Pardon?"

Oh God. Had she said that out loud?

Dalton slid his hand around her waist, and to her utter mortification, the tenderness in his touch nearly made her weep. "Why don't we go sit down?"

"Wait." Artem held out a hand. "Can I have a word with you, brother?"

Dalton gave a terse shake of his head. "There's no time. The show is about to start."

"Diana's class doesn't compete for another half hour. Why don't we go fetch drinks for the ladies and discuss a little business as well?" Artem's mouth curved into one of his charming smiles, but his eyes went dark.

Dalton sighed under his breath. "Very well. If it absolutely can't wait…"

"It can't." Artem reached for Ophelia's hand, gave it a squeeze. "Darling, why don't you show Aurélie around for few minutes?"

Ophelia slipped a willowy arm through Aurélie's. "I'd be happy to. Artem's right. The show doesn't technically start until ten o'clock. It's only 9:30."

9:30.

If it was 9:30 in New York right now, that meant it

was 3:30 in Delamotte. Her portrait sitting with Lord Clement was scheduled in less than an hour.

She swallowed.

Across the world, her gold dress was no doubt hanging in her dressing room with her glittering silver Jimmy Choos set out beside it. The Marchand family tiara would have been removed from its vault. Her old life was ready and waiting for her to slip back into it.

Like a dress that no longer fit.

Once they were out of earshot, Dalton didn't bother waiting for Artem to speak. He knew what was coming.

"Again, this isn't how it looks," he muttered under his breath as they fell in line at the bar.

"So you've mentioned," Artem said drily.

Clearly, Artem didn't believe him. Maybe because this time things were *exactly* how they looked.

Dalton's jaw clenched. A dull throb started up in his temples. He shouldn't have brought Aurélie here. It had been a mistake. Obviously.

Dalton didn't make mistakes. Not when it came to business. Rather, he hadn't until the past twelve hours or so.

Now he couldn't seem to stop.

And he'd tried. By God, he'd tried to get a handle on himself.

He'd intentionally spent the better part of the three-hour ride to the Hamptons on his laptop rather than interacting with Aurélie. He was woefully behind on plans for the Drake Diamonds gala. Mrs. Barnes had emailed him three menu options for review, along with photographs of floral arrangements in various sizes and shades of Drake blue, and she'd been pressing him for a response for days. He hadn't even given the guest list a cursory glance since the invitations had been mailed out. And of course the most important detail still required his attention—the arrangement of the Marchand eggs.

As much as he'd told himself he was simply doing his job, Dalton knew better. He'd wanted the distraction. Needed it. Because having Aurélie situated right beside him in the backseat of the town car, wearing another one of her quirky vintage getups, was killing him.

There was the faintest hint of lace peeking out from the hem of her dress today, and her legs were covered in opaque tights. Or perhaps they were stockings... Dalton had spent far too much time pondering the possibility of a garter belt beneath the swish of her full skirts. There wasn't a big enough distraction in the world to rid himself of his curiosity regarding that particular matter. It had consumed the majority of his thoughts during the entire stretch of I-495.

And then there'd been the matter of the email.

Less than an hour away from Manhattan, Dalton's tablet had dinged, indicating he'd gotten a new email. He'd glanced at the notification and his gut had tied itself in knots.

From: The Office of His Majesty,
The Reigning Prince, Delamotte
Re: Her Royal Highness, Aurélie Marchand

He'd switched the tablet off before Aurélie could see it. There was no reason to alarm her until he'd had a chance to read the message. It didn't necessarily mean they'd figured out where she'd gone.

But things didn't look promising. His fists clenched

at his sides and he cursed himself—yet again—for not sending her home last night. Last night...before things had gotten so carried away. Before he'd danced with her in the street. Before she'd undressed for him in that shaft of immaculate moonlight.

He'd remember how it felt to look at her beautiful body for the first time until the day he died. Like time had somehow reversed itself. He'd felt young again. Alive. Whole.

Artem stared at him long and hard, turning his back on the course where the riders and horses were warming up, preparing for competition. He shook his head and sighed. "When are you going to admit what's going on, brother?"

Dalton shrugged. "There's nothing to admit."

It was a half truth, at best. At worst, a full-fledged lie. Dalton had so much to confess where Aurélie was concerned that he'd lost track. But he didn't care to discuss it. Especially not with Artem, whom Dalton had so often chastised for failing to control his libido. The day his brother had slipped a diamond on Ophelia's hand, he'd become a different person.

Maybe you can become a different man, too.

"Who is it you're trying to fool?" Artem said. "Me? Or yourself?"

"The exhibit is going forward as scheduled. I have things under control." But that wasn't even the whole truth, was it? He still had no idea what was in the email from the palace. Even now, the cell phone in his pocket vibrated against his leg.

He reached for it and checked the screen. Incoming call: Drake Diamonds. Whatever was happening at the store could wait. For now.

He powered down the phone and slid it back in his pocket. He was having enough trouble concentrating on what was happening around him today as it was.

He took a deep breath and refocused his attention on Artem, who was still standing there. Watching. Waiting. Apparently, he wasn't going to let the Aurélie thing go.

Dalton cleared his throat. "Look, I appreciate your concern, brother. But I don't need a heart-to-heart about my sex life."

He wouldn't be taking Aurélie to bed again, anyway. His feelings on the subject no longer mattered.

Except they did matter. The fact that he couldn't stop thinking about that damned suitcase told him his feelings mattered a whole hell of a lot.

Aurélie should have been back in Delamotte by now. He'd lain awake half the night trying to figure out why he hadn't put her on the plane when he'd had every intention of doing so, and he'd been unable to come up with anything remotely resembling a logical explanation. Then again, the decadent sight of Aurélie naked in his bed might have had something to do with his inability to think.

It had taken every shred of self-control in his arsenal not to kiss her, to touch her—right here, right now—when every time he closed his eyes he saw her sitting astride him, heavy-lidded with desire.

"I'm not talking about sex," Artem said. "You have feelings for Aurélie."

Dalton couldn't believe what he was hearing. "Don't be ridiculous."

Artem rolled his eyes. "I'm not the one being ridiculous here. You're in love with her. Ophelia sees it. I see it. Why can't you?"

"Listen, I'm happy for the two of you, happy about the baby. Thrilled. Delighted. But just because you've suddenly become a family man doesn't mean I'm one."

"But you are. You always have been." Artem threw his hands up. "Look around, for crying out loud. You're at a horse show."

Dalton didn't need to look around. He knew perfectly well where he was. The Winter Hamptons Equestrian Classic was an off-season event, although most serious jumpers like Diana competed year-round. Diana participated twelve months a year, and since both their parents were now deceased, Dalton tried to attend every show within driving distance of Manhattan.

Not that their father had ever displayed much interest in his only daughter before his fatal heart attack. Geoffrey Drake had been writing checks since Diana began taking riding lessons at the age of four, but that had been the extent of his support for her career. He'd never attended a single horse show.

As far as Dalton knew, his sister hadn't considered this at all strange. The Drakes had always expressed affection via their checkbooks, after all.

Family man. Right. Dalton didn't even know what a family man looked like.

Dalton himself had never seen Diana ride until after Clarissa died. To this day, he wasn't sure why he'd turned up in the grandstand at that first show he'd attended. Maybe he'd been looking for an escape. Maybe he'd simply needed a place to go on Sunday morning before the store opened in those early days when he couldn't bear the stark white interior of his apartment.

He wasn't sure. All he knew was that it had made him feel better knowing that at least one Drake had managed to build a life that didn't revolve around the family business. He would have gladly flung himself on Diamond's back and galloped far away if he could.

If it hadn't been too late.

If he hadn't already devoted his entire existence to Drake Diamonds.

"You deserve to be happy, Dalton. Whatever is happening between you and Aurélie has nothing to do with the past." Artem's gaze shifted to the packed dirt floor. "It's got nothing to do with Clarissa."

Dalton glared at his brother. "You're out of line. And for what it's worth, categorically wrong."

You're in love with her.

In love?

Impossible.

He wanted Aurélie. He didn't love her. There was a difference. A big one.

Falling in love with Aurélie Marchand would make him the biggest idiot on the island of Manhattan. Possibly even the entire continent.

Although if he was being honest with himself, he *had* been acting rather idiotic lately.

"I'm wrong, am I?" Artem glanced at the box where Ophelia and Aurélie were chatting with each other like two old friends. Like sisters. "Then why haven't you sent the princess packing?"

Dalton wished he knew why. Oh, how he wished that.

Chapter Twelve

Aurélie did her best to make conversation with Ophelia as they sat in the Drake Diamonds private box in the front row. She listened patiently to Ophelia's explanation of the rules of showjumping, nodding in all the right places and making note of which riders were serious contenders for the Winter Hamptons Equestrian Classic Grand Prix title.

Diana was one of them. Dalton's sister rode with a passionate confidence that took Aurélie's breath away, as if she and the horse were one.

But as she followed their movements around the ring during the warm-up and Ophelia kept up her merry chit-chatting, Aurélie couldn't shake the knowledge of what was going on 4,000 miles away.

Her time was up.

Palace officials may have discovered her absence earlier this morning. In all likelihood, they had. Perhaps even yesterday. But so long as Aurélie didn't know for certain, she could hold onto the hope that she was still flying under the radar. She could choose to believe that no one would come looking for her. But once Lord Clement arrived at the palace, there would be no denying the truth. In just a few short minutes, she'd no longer be able to lie to herself.

No matter how badly she wanted to.

She couldn't stop glancing at the digital time display beside the judge's table, couldn't stop herself from counting down each minute, each precious second of freedom. Yet, she felt oddly calm. The minutes ticked by, and her pulse remained steady. There were no nervous butterflies, no panicked heartbeats. On the contrary, a detached serenity seemed to come over her.

She was dangerously calm. Numb. So much so that it frightened her.

"I wonder what's taking Artem and Dalton so long. The show is about to start, and Diana and Diamond are the first team up." Ophelia glanced around the crowded tent. "Do you see them anywhere?"

Aurélie scanned the area by the bar, and spotted them on the way to the box. Both of them carried a champagne glass in each hand, and both of them wore grim expressions. Although Dalton's was significantly grimmer than Artem's.

"Here they come," she said.

The closer they came, the clearer she could discern the barely contained fury in Dalton's posture. She wondered if something terrible had happened back at the store. A robbery perhaps.

Or maybe…

No. She shook her head, unwilling to even consider the possibility that the palace had somehow already found out where she was. *Not that. Please not that.*

She still had a few minutes left until the palace realized she was missing. At least she thought she did.

Artem's expression softened the moment he set eyes on his wife again. He handed a glass to Ophelia and winked. "It's just water, darling. But I had them put it in a fancy glass for you."

"Thank you." They exchanged a kiss that lasted just long enough to make Aurélie clear her throat and look away.

Dalton took the seat beside her. "Your champagne."

Bubbles rose from the pale gold liquid in the glass that Dalton handed her—a saucer-style glass with a delicate stem. A *Marie Antoinette glass*, as it was known in Delamotte.

Stop. Just stop.

She vowed to quit thinking about Delamotte and what might be going on back at the palace, yet still found herself lapsing into French. *"Merci beaucoup."*

Dalton barely looked at her. He kept his gaze glued straight ahead, yet didn't seem to follow the gallop of Diamond's hooves as the horse swept a wide loop around the course. His jaw hardened into a firm line.

Something was definitely wrong.

She glanced at the clock again. 9:58.

Two more minutes.

She took a large gulp from her champagne glass and slid her gaze toward Dalton. "Is everything okay?"

"Fine," he said under his breath.

"Clearly." She took another sip of champagne and watched Diana trot into the ring on Diamond's back.

The buzzer rang, signaling the start of her run, and Diamond shot forward in a cloud of red dust. His glossy black tail streamed straight out behind him. The ground shook as he thundered past the Drake box.

Horse and rider soared over the first jump, clearing the rails by such a large height that it looked like they were flying. Diana rose out of the saddle and leaned forward. Aurélie could see the dazzling smile on her face clear across the ring.

What must it feel like to be that fearless? She wished she knew. "Wow."

Her heart leaped to her throat as they approached the second obstacle, which was a water jump. Diamond soared over the partition and then seemed to hang suspended over the glistening pool. Without thinking, Aurélie gripped Dalton's arm and held her breath until the horse touched down gracefully on the other side.

She let out a relieved exhale. Then she realized she was still holding onto Dalton's sleeve.

Her face went hot. "Sorry." She let go. "You don't get nervous watching Diana ride?"

"No. She's an excellent competitor," he said stiffly.

Okay then.

Diana and Diamond galloped past the box again. Artem, Ophelia and Aurélie all cheered while Dalton remained silent.

Aurélie stared at him. "Are you sure everything is okay?" *Other than the fact that we slept together last night and today has been awkward on every possible level.* "Because you seem awfully cranky all of a sudden. Even for you, I mean."

"Quite sure. Artem can be a real pain in my ass sometimes. That's all," he said.

Then he turned and looked at her. *Really* looked at her for the first time since he'd sat down. Possibly even for the first time since she'd so bluntly informed him that she wouldn't be sleeping with him again.

His gaze softened, and his mouth curved into a smile. But it was a sad smile. Bittersweet. All at once, memories from the night before came flooding back—the reverent expression on his face as her dress fell to the floor, the tenderness of his lips on her breasts, the exquisite fullness as he'd entered her. Tears gathered behind Aurélie's eyes, and he said, "Then again, every once in a while my brother is right about some things."

She bit her lip to keep from crying, blinked furiously and did her best to keep her attention on the ring where Diamond was gathering his front legs beneath him to soar over another set of rails. But Dalton's gaze was a palpable force.

She turned to him again.

"Dalton." Her voice was a broken whisper.

He cupped her cheek. "Princess."

And for the briefest of seconds, she felt it again—the tenuous connection they'd shared the night before, as precious as a diaphanous dream.

It was real. This *is real.*

A hush fell over her heart, and in that sliver of a moment, everything slipped softly into place. There was no faraway palace, no royal wedding. Just him. Just her. *Just us.*

Then a tinny clang pierced the quiet and it all fell apart. Like pearls slipping from a string.

Dalton seemed to realize something was wrong before he saw it. His smile faded, lips compressed. In the final moment their eyes were still locked, Aurélie saw fear in his gaze. Raw, primal fear that made her blood run cold.

Her throat went dry, and she realized the sound she'd heard had been Diamond's front hooves hitting the rail.

Diana.

The world seemed to move in slow motion as Aurélie's head swiveled in the direction of the course. Already Dalton was scrambling to his feet, climbing out of the box, as the horse's back feet sent the rails flying and the big, graceful animal crashed into the dirt with a sickening thud. He hit the ground with such force that Aurélie's chair pitched forward and she had to grab onto the railing in front of her to keep herself from falling.

Diamond's leg twisted into a horrific angle, and a terrible sound came out of him. A sound that would haunt Aurélie's dreams for weeks to come. She wanted to close her eyes, to block it all out. But she couldn't. Not until she found Dalton's sister in the wreckage.

The horse tried to scramble to his feet, and when he did, Diana's petite form rolled out of the way.

She's okay. She's all right.

But Diamond couldn't support himself on his broken leg and fell sideways, his big, beautiful head smacking down squarely on top of Diana's helmet.

Her body went limp. A gasp went up from the crowd. Time sped up again and somewhere in the periphery, Aurélie was vaguely aware of the clock flashing 10:00.

"Oh, my god." Ophelia's hand flew to her throat.

"Let's go," Artem said, helping Ophelia up.

Aurélie wasn't sure if she should follow or stay put, but Ophelia grabbed her hand and held on tight as she walked past. So she followed the two of them out of the box and to the entrance to the ring, where Dalton stood as pale as a ghost.

"I'm so sorry, Dalton. She'll be okay. She will," Aurélie said, knowing full well it might be a lie.

But sometimes people needed to believe in lies, didn't they? Sometimes a lie was the only thing that kept a person going. At least that was what Aurélie's mother had written in her diary.

She swallowed, not quite sure what to believe anymore.

Diana was already surrounded by EMTs, since qualified medical personnel were required to be on hand at all equestrian events that included showjumping. A siren wailed in the distance, and Artem was talking in terse tones to the show chairman, worried that the ambulance would have trouble reaching the tent through the maze of horse trailers and cars parked outside in the snow.

Through the chaos, Dalton remained stoic. He didn't move, didn't say a word. He scarcely seemed to breathe.

When at last Diana had been lifted into the back of an ambulance—strapped onto a gurney with her head still in its riding helmet—Dalton seemed surprised to find Aurélie standing beside him. It was as if he'd been in a trance and forgotten she was there.

"Come with me." He placed his hand in the small of her back and escorted her out of the tent, to the edge of the parking lot where two sleek black cars sat idling, waiting to follow the ambulance to the hospital.

The sky had turned an ominous gray, heavy with snow. The cold air hit Aurélie's face like a slap. She ducked her head against the wind.

"We'll meet you there," Artem called, nodding solemnly as he and Ophelia climbed into the back of a sedan.

Dalton nodded and held the door open to the town car. Aurélie slid inside and scooted across the seat to make room for him. But he didn't get in right away. Instead he leaned into the opened window and murmured something to the driver.

"Yes, sir," the chauffeur said and shifted the car into Drive.

What was happening?

"Wait!" Aurélie scrambled to open the door.

"*Miss*," the driver said in a firm tone. "Mr. Drake has given me instructions…"

She didn't wait for him to finish. She pushed her way out of the car and ran to catch up with Dalton, who'd already begun walking away.

"Where are you going?" She could hear the panic in her own voice, but she didn't care how desperate it sounded. Didn't care how desperate she looked, slipping and sliding on the icy pavement. Because she knew what he was going to say before he even turned around.

"Aurélie." He gripped her shoulders and held her at arm's length. "Get back in the car."

She shook her head and opened her mouth to object, but no words would come out. They stuck in her throat. She couldn't seem to make a sound.

Dalton's expression hardened, and she was hit with the realization that it didn't matter what she said. Or what she didn't. There were no words that could make him change his mind.

"I want you to go, Aurélie," he said, and she wished with her whole heart that he would call her princess again. Just one more time. "Go home."

Home.

The word hung in the space between them, ominous with meaning.

He wasn't talking about his apartment back in Manhattan. He didn't mean *his* home. He meant *hers*. Delamotte.

"I can't go, Dalton. Not now." How could he expect her to walk away at a time like this?

"I'm not asking you, Aurélie. I'm telling you." He paused, took a deep breath. He suddenly didn't look so stoic anymore. Or angry, either. Just tired. So very tired.

"I want you to go. It's time."

Chapter Thirteen

Dalton hadn't set foot in a hospital since the day Clarissa died.

He'd managed to avoid the beeping machines, the drawn curtains, the memories steeped in antiseptic perfume for six long years. Even in the wake of his father's heart attack, he'd stayed away. At the time, it had been alarmingly easy to explain his absence as a necessity. While Diana sat vigil at their father's bedside and Artem had gone MIA doing God knows what, no one had actually expected Dalton to show up.

They'd expected him to be sitting at his desk. Just like always. It was what their father would have wanted, after all. This expectation had of course been partially instrumental in the events causing Dalton to despise hospitals to begin with.

Oh, the irony.

Dalton had been at the office until 2 a.m. the night Clarissa slit her wrists. What no one knew, either then or now, was that he'd put away his spreadsheets and emails sometime around 10 p.m. After scrolling through all the notifications of Clarissa's missed calls on his cell, he'd opted to sleep on the sofa in his office rather than going home.

He hadn't been in the mood for another argument about his work schedule. Or his inattentiveness. Or anything, really. Whatever feelings he'd had for Clarissa had long since faded. He'd been going through the motions for months. A year perhaps. He just hadn't gotten around to officially breaking things off, in part because he'd had too much on his plate at Drake Diamonds. But mainly because Geoffrey Drake would have been livid when he found out Dalton was calling off his engagement. It had been his father's plan all along to have Clarissa join the Drake dynasty with the diamond empire her grandfather ran.

And like the obedient son that he'd always been, Dalton had fallen into step.

Until he couldn't.

He didn't love her. He was quite sure she didn't love him, either. They'd been thrown together like two animals in a cage, and each in their own way, they'd begun fighting for a way out.

With hindsight had come the benefit of clarity. Dalton could see the arguments, the tantrums, even the suicide, for what they were. Clarissa had wanted to escape. And she'd done just that.

Nevertheless, knowing why she'd done it hadn't lifted the mantle of regret. Dalton should have seen what was happening. He'd always prided himself on his attention to detail, his keen sense of accountability. Whether they'd loved each other or not, Clarissa had been his fiancée. His responsibility. He should have gotten her the help that she needed.

He should have picked up the godforsaken phone.

Instead, he'd woken up sometime in the middle of the night and finally headed home. But only after checking his phone first and seeing that the calls had stopped. He'd assumed Clarissa had finally given up and gone to bed. He wished to hell and back that he'd been right. He wished so many things.

"Mr. Drake, your sister's room is right this way." A nurse wearing mint-green scrubs and holding a clipboard led him down a corridor on the third floor of Southampton Hospital.

Dalton fell in step behind her.

A sign on the wall announced he was in the Head Trauma unit. Just up ahead, Dalton saw a young man in a wheelchair with his skull immobilized in a halo brace, eyes staring blankly into space. He couldn't have been more than sixteen or seventeen years old. Dalton dropped his gaze to the nurse's feet in front of him and her soft-soled white shoes padding silently down the hospital corridor.

"Here we are." She stopped in front of a closed door. Room 367.

She extended a hand to push the door open, and Dalton stopped her. "Wait. Before we go in…"

"Yes?" She smiled politely at him, her kind eyes full of concern. She was being so nice. Everyone was. The paramedics. The ambulance driver. Even the damn Uber driver who'd come to pick him up at the horse show.

It made Dalton want to scream.

"How bad is it?" he asked, hating himself for sounding so desperate.

Clarissa's death should have prepared him for this. What good was the cement wall he'd so carefully constructed around his soul if it didn't protect him from falling apart in the face of tragedy?

"We're still waiting on the results of the CT scan, so I'm afraid I can't really say. She's conscious, and that's a great sign. Her head hurts, though, so she's drifting in and out. The doctor should be in to speak with you shortly. In the meantime, Diana is resting comfortably. Her monitors will alert us if her vital signs change. But if you need anything—anything at all—we're right down the hall, Mr. Drake." She smiled again. Too big. Too nauseatingly nice.

"Very well. I understand." He nodded, and pushed the door open himself, needing to feel as in control of the situation as he could.

As if such an idea were remotely possible.

The nurse checked the beeping machine by Diana's bed and made a few notations on her clipboard while Dalton shifted his weight uncomfortably from one foot to the other. The room was huge. Private. What good was all that time spent at the office if the Drake money couldn't be put to good use? The sheer size of it, along with the huge bay window overlooking the beachfront of Southampton, made the mechanical hospital bed in the center of the room seem absurdly tiny. Resting in a hospital gown and sterile white sheets with her eyes shut tight, Diana looked pale and dainty.

Dainty was a word Dalton had never associated with his sister before. *Strong*, yes. *Fearless*, most definitely. *Dainty* had never been part of the equation.

Even now, it didn't seem right. Dalton frowned, struggling for the right adjective. It was a relief to have something to concentrate on. Something concrete and logical. Until he realized the word he was looking for was *broken*.

His chest seized, and he let out a cough.

The nurse rested a comforting hand on his shoulder. "Give us a shout if you or your sister need anything."

Her voice was a soothing whisper. Dalton nodded, wondering when he'd sunk into the overstuffed leather recliner at Diana's bedside. He had no memory of it. Nor of taking his sister's hand in his own. He wondered if he might be in shock, medically speaking. Not that it mattered. Only one thing mattered right now, and it most definitely wasn't him.

Wake up.

He'd feel a lot better about her prognosis if she'd simply open her eyes. He didn't say it aloud, though. He didn't dare, lest it come out as harshly as it sounded in his head.

Wake the hell up.

Dalton didn't want to be that guy—the angry one screaming orders at an unconscious young woman. Even though deep down, he knew that was exactly who he was. The moment Diana's horse went down, the second his hooves hit the rail and his slender ebony legs buckled beneath him, something had come unwound inside Dalton. Something dark and ugly.

Anger.

Six years of bloody, blinding anger that he'd buried in numbers and sales figures and marketing strategies. But like a diamond buried in a mine, his fury hadn't crumbled during its time in the darkness. It had grown exponentially sharper. Stronger. Dazzling in its intensity.

She wasn't in a coma. She'd been alert when they'd taken her away in the ambulance. She needed rest. He knew that.

But once she'd closed her eyes, Dalton worried they wouldn't open again. After all, that's what had happened last time he sat beside a hospital bed.

His fists clenched in his lap. He was furious. Furious at the horse. Furious at Diana and whatever terrible impulse drove her to hurl herself in harm's way over and over and over again. He was even furious at poor Clarissa.

And his father. Always.

Was there anyone he wasn't angry at?

Unbidden, Aurélie's lovely face came to mind. The pull of the memory was irresistible, dragging him under. He closed his eyes and let himself drown. Just for a moment. Just long enough to summon her generous lips and the elegant curve of her neck. Regal. Classic. A neck made for ropes and ropes of pearls.

But then he remembered her expression when she'd climbed out of the car and come running after him—the bewildered hurt in her emerald eyes, coupled with the painful knowledge that such damage had been his doing.

He opened his eyes and pushed the memory back into place.

I want you to go, Aurélie. It's time.

It had been past time for her to return to Delamotte, gala or no gala. He'd done the right thing.

For both of them.

Then why does it feel so wrong?

"Dalton?"

His heart crashed to a stop. He blinked in relief at the sight of Diana's opened eyes, wide and searching.

He forced himself to smile. "You're awake."

"I am." She nodded, winced and closed her eyes again. "My head hurts. I keep drifting off."

"It's okay. I'm here." He gave her hand a reassuring squeeze.

There was a smudge of red clay on one of Diana's cheeks. Dirt from the riding arena. He wiped it away with a brush of his thumb and pondered the fact that they hadn't cleaned her up. Yet there was a startling lack of blood, given the seriousness of her condition. She didn't have so much as a bruise.

Relief flooded through Dalton's veins and he swallowed. Hard. He could taste the rusty fragrance of blood in his mouth, a sensory memory of the last time he'd sat at a bedside like this one.

With Clarissa, there'd been so much blood. Red everywhere. Afterward, he'd had the apartment painted top to bottom and all the furniture replaced with nothing but white.

Again, his thoughts drifted to Aurélie. Aurélie, with her porcelain skin and windswept hair. Aurélie, swaying to Gershwin in his arms. Aurélie, adopting a dog on a whim. The ugliest one of the bunch.

He shouldn't be thinking of her at a time like this. He shouldn't be thinking of her at all. She didn't have anything to do with his family or his life. She was business. She was temporary. She was royal, for God's sake.

Yet when Diamond's hooves hit the rail with a sickening clang, when he'd watched his sister's head slam into the ground, Aurélie had been the one he'd wanted at his side. Not wanted. Needed. Needed with a ferocity that terrified him.

He didn't want to need anyone, least of all a princess.

You're in love with her. Ophelia sees it. I see it. Why can't you?

Dalton half believed Artem had been joking. Maybe. Maybe not. But his words had touched a nerve.

Out of the question.

He couldn't have feelings for Aurélie. Absolutely not. Not before Diana's accident, and most definitely not now. Not when he'd been reminded so vividly of all the reasons why he was better off on his own.

He wasn't made for this. He never had been. He was his father's son, through and through.

The door swung open again. Dalton turned, hoping with every fiber of his being to find a doctor standing in the doorway. A shining beacon of hope. Instead, he took in the tear-stained face of his sister-in-law, followed closely by his brother.

He dropped Diana's hand and stood. "Artem. Ophelia."

"Dalton?" Ophelia's brow furrowed. "How on earth did you get here so fast?"

"I gave the driver an incentive to get me here in a hurry." Again, the Drake money had come in handy.

"Marvelous." Artem rolled his eyes. "Don't you think we've had enough accidents for one day?"

"I got here in one piece, didn't I?"

"Stop. Both of you." Ophelia's voice wobbled a little. Great. He'd reduced a pregnant woman to tears. That might be a new low, even for Dalton. "This isn't the time for bickering. Diana needs us. All of us."

Diana needs us.

Dalton sank back into the chair and dropped his head in his hands. He wanted to tear his hair out by the roots. The door opened again, and it took superhuman effort for him to look up.

A man wearing green scrubs entered the room and extended his hand. "Hello, I'm Dr. Chris Larson."

Dalton shot to his feet. "Doctor."

Artem and Ophelia introduced themselves, then Dr. Larson cut to the chase. "I have the results from your sister's tests. As you know, she took a nasty spill. Fortunately, she was wearing a helmet. A good one, by all appearances."

This came as a relief, but not as a surprise, to Dalton. As fearless as Diana was, she'd always played by the rules. She had ambition, not a death wish.

The doctor nodded. "It looks like the safety precaution did its job."

Dalton frowned. "Are you sure? She's lying in a hospital bed and can barely keep her eyes open."

"Diana is suffering from a concussion, which is to be expected after taking a hit the way she did. But she's going to be fine. I'm sure she's got a monster of a headache, but now that we know there's no permanent damage, we can start administering something stronger than Tylenol. Still, we'll want to keep an eye on her at least overnight. We'll take her vitals every hour and make sure she's doing well. But those should be precautions. Barring any unforeseen complications, I expect your sister to make a full recovery."

"Thank goodness," Ophelia said. Artem wrapped his arm around her and pulled her close.

"A full recovery?" Dalton tried to focus on the doctor's face, but he couldn't seem to tear his gaze from his sister. "You're sure?"

The doctor nodded. "The scans show no structural damage to the brain tissue. She needs time to rest, but soon she'll be able to do all the things she loves to do. Including showjumping."

"That might be a tough call," Artem said under his breath. "Her horse had to be put down today."

Dalton's gut clenched. He hadn't known what happened to the horse. He'd been so worried about Diana that he hadn't even asked about the animal.

Diamond was dead. *Shit.*

His sister would be devastated. Dalton sighed and wished he could go one day, just one, without thinking about loss. Then again, he had, hadn't he? While Aurélie had been there, he'd been able to let go. Just a little bit.

He'd lived.

And now she's gone, too.

"So what happens next?" Artem asked.

The doctor assured them the hospital staff was doing everything it could to make Diana's stay comfortable. He'd given instructions for the night nurse to call him if anything changed.

Diana woke up briefly. Just long enough to register Artem and Ophelia's presence and to answer a few questions for Dr. Larson.

When her eyes fluttered closed again, he gave her arm a pat. "You're a lucky girl, Miss Drake."

Dalton knew the doctor was right. Diana had been lucky indeed, but he doubted she'd see it that way when she found out Diamond was dead. Part of him wondered if she'd avoided asking about her horse because deep down she knew.

They all knew.

No matter how things looked on the outside, the Drakes had never had luck on their side.

Aurélie sat in the backseat, still trying to absorb Dalton's words as the snowy stretch of Long Island flew past the car windows in a melancholy blur.

I'm not asking you, Aurélie. I'm telling you. I want you to go. It's time.

How could she leave without knowing if Diana was going to be okay? And the horse?

And Dalton.

He didn't mean it. He couldn't.

He'd sure sounded like he meant it, though. Everything about his tone, his stance and the glittering determination in his gaze had been resolute. He'd made up his mind. He wanted her gone.

She had to leave, obviously. She couldn't stay. Not now.

Even if she did, what could she possibly do to help? Her presence would only do more harm than good.

Aurélie had never felt so useless in her entire life, which struck her as profoundly ironic considering she was a princess. She should have been accustomed to not being particularly useful by now, especially in view of the fact that the last time she'd had any communication with the palace, they hadn't even noticed she'd fled the country.

Surely they've noticed now.

It was nearly 6 p.m. in Delamotte. Lord Clement had no doubt come and gone in a royal huff. Everyone would be looking for her, including the Crown Prince.

Any temptation to put the SIM card back in her cell

phone and check her messages had died the moment Diana's horse went down. Aurélie couldn't think about the palace right now. Or her impending engagement. Or even her father. All those people, all those worries, seemed so inconsequential compared to what she'd just witnessed. How could she possibly be thinking about something as silly as a press release after seeing Dalton's sister fall headfirst to the ground?

She couldn't.

Aurélie squeezed her eyes closed and leaned her head against the backseat of the town car. The fall kept running through her mind in an endless loop of catastrophic images and terrible sounds. The thunder of hooves. The thud of Diamond's elegant legs crashing into the rails. Those same slender bones buckling and twisting into unnatural angles. Diana's helmet bouncing on the packed red clay.

But worse than the fall itself had been the look on Dalton's face when his sister failed to get up. In a shadow of a moment, Aurélie had seen a lifetime of pain etched in the lines around his eyes. Stories he'd never told her, never would. Something had happened to Dalton Drake. Something terrible.

Diana had to be okay. She *had* to.

Aurélie would have given everything she had to be at the hospital with the Drakes, but Dalton had made his wishes clear when he put her in the town car.

He doesn't want you there.

He doesn't want you. Period.

It stung. Aurélie knew it shouldn't. She wasn't one of them. She and Dalton weren't a couple. They were two people who'd been thrown together for a few days. Nothing more.

And now she had no idea what was going on, what had become of his sister or even the injured horse. Not knowing was torture. She thought about asking the driver if she could borrow his phone, but decided against it. If Dalton wanted to get in touch with her, he would.

Aurélie spent the entire ride back to the city in agonizing silence. At last the steely skyscrapers of Manhattan came into view. "Can you drop me at Drake Diamonds before we go back to the apartment?"

She no longer wanted the secret egg. Dalton could keep it for all she cared. She hated it now, hated what it stood for—the cheating, the lies. The egg had served its purpose. It had gotten her a few days of freedom. It was her bargaining chip, and now the bargain was over.

But her mother's pearls were at the store. Dalton had given them to Ophelia to be restrung. The last time Aurélie had seen them, they'd been lined up on a velvet tray on Ophelia's desk.

She prayed they were still there.

"Very well." The car rolled past the horse carriages lined up on the curb by Central Park and turned onto Fifth Avenue.

They passed the elegant entrance to the Plaza Hotel and too soon, the imposing façade of Drake Diamonds came into view.

"Thank you." Aurélie climbed out and paused in front of the store, blinking against the snow flurries drifting from the dove-gray sky.

Just walk inside, get your pearls back and then you can go home and put all of this behind you.

Her feet refused to move. It felt strange being here without Dalton. Wrong, somehow.

This had been a mistake. She would just ring Mrs.

Barnes when she got back to Delamotte and ask her to return the pearls by post.

She turned to get back in the car, but it had already been swallowed up in the steady stream of yellow cabs snaking their way through upper Manhattan. That's right. Even Dalton's driver couldn't just park by the curb indefinitely.

She considered staying put and waiting for him to make a loop around the block and return. It could take mere minutes. Or, given the erratic nature of New York traffic, she could be stuck standing here for half an hour.

Okay then. She took a deep breath, turned and pushed through the revolving doors.

"Oh, thank goodness." Mrs. Barnes pounced on Aurélie the moment her kitten heels hit the showroom floor. "Where's Mr. Drake?"

Aurélie blinked. "Dalton?"

"Yes." Mrs. Barnes, whom Aurélie had never seen with even a single hair out of place, looked borderline frantic. She shook her head and tossed her hands up in the air. "Or Artem. Or Ophelia. Any of the Drakes, for that matter. I've been calling all three of them for hours and can't reach anyone."

Aurélie wasn't sure how much she should divulge. It didn't appear as though Dalton's assistant knew about Diana's accident. Or maybe she did, and was hoping for more information about Diana's condition. "They're… um…unreachable at the moment."

"Yes, I know. They're in the Hamptons. But I need to speak to Mr. Drake. Now." Barnes's gaze narrowed. "I'd assumed he was with you."

"No." She shook her head. Clearly Mrs. Barnes didn't

know what was going on, and it wasn't Aurélie's place to tell her. "Is there a problem?"

"You could say that, yes. A multitude of problems, actually. We were so busy that we had lunch brought in for the staff this afternoon, and now half of them have fallen ill with food poisoning. The store has never been this shortstaffed."

"Oh, no. That's terrible."

"I've been working the sales floor all afternoon." She waved a hand around the showroom, which upon closer inspection, had a rather frantic air about it. "I've tied over 400 white bows since two o'clock."

"What can I do to help?" Aurélie knew nothing about selling diamonds. Or anything else about working at a jewelry store. But she could learn. And she was pretty sure she could tie a bow.

Mrs. Barnes eyed her with no small amount of skepticism.

"Seriously, I want to help." *Please, let me.* It was a chance to be useful for once in her life. At a time when she needed it most of all.

Mrs. Barnes's apology was swift. "No, no, no. You're Mr. Drake's guest. That's not necessary."

"From what you said, it sounds very necessary." Even an ocean away from Delamotte, people still didn't think she was capable of doing anything useful. It made Aurélie want to scream. "Please. *Please.* I'll do anything."

Dalton's secretary bit her lip and looked Aurélie up and down. "Anything?"

"Yes." Aurélie nodded furiously. "You name it."

"Okay. I hope I don't get fired for this, but they're absolutely desperate for help upstairs. Anything you could do up there would be appreciated."

Aurélie swallowed. "Upstairs?" A trickle of dread snaked its way up her spine.

Mrs. Barnes flicked a hand toward the ceiling. "In Engagements."

Not that. Anything but Engagements.

She'd rather clean the toilets than spend the rest of the day neck-deep in diamond engagement rings.

But what could she possibly say? She'd begged to help. Refusing would mean everyone was right about her. Her father. Dalton. And as much as she hated to admit it, even herself. How could she fight her destiny if she couldn't even make herself get off the elevator on the tenth floor?

"I think every bride and groom in the city decided to shop for rings today," Mrs. Barnes said. *Oh joy.* "They need champagne. And petit fours. And gift wrapping. Find the floor manager, and he'll put you to work."

"Right." Aurélie nodded.

She could do this. Couldn't she?

"I'll be up to check on you in a bit."

Aurélie watched as Mrs. Barnes crossed the showroom floor with purpose in her stride. It would have been so easy to turn around and walk back out the revolving door. So easy to get back in the car, collect Jacques from the pet sitter at Dalton's apartment and head straight to the airport.

Too easy.

She'd had enough of taking the easy way out. She squared her shoulders, marched straight toward the elevator and stepped inside.

"Tenth floor, *s'il vous plait*," she told the elevator attendant.

He eyed her warily. Not that she could blame him. "Yes, ma'am."

The elevator doors swished closed. When they opened again, she exited as swiftly as possible. Maybe she could simply outrun her panic.

Then again, maybe not. As soon as she found herself surrounded by the glass cases of sparkling diamond solitaires, the familiar tightness gathered in her chest. Her knees went wobbly, and she had trouble catching her breath. Aurélie squeezed her eyes shut, and when she did, she no longer saw herself in a white gown walking down the aisle of the grand cathedral in Delamotte. Her recurrent nightmare had been replaced. Instead, she saw Diamond barreling toward the double-rail jump. She saw him stumble and fall. She saw Diana slamming into the ground headfirst.

Aurélie's eyes flew open. This was absurd. Diana was lying in a hospital bed, possibly even fighting for her life. Surely Aurélie could tolerate a few giddy brides and grooms.

There were more than a few. There were dozens. Under the direction of the acting floor manager, Aurélie brought them flutes of champagne. She served them cake. She oohed and ahed as they tried on rings. She offered her congratulations, wrapped more rings than she could count in little Drake-blue boxes and tied white bows.

And it wasn't altogether terrible.

Granted, she got a little misty eyed if she paid too much attention to the way the grooms looked at their brides-to-be. So much unabashed adoration was a little much to take, especially when she almost allowed herself to believe Dalton had looked at her in the same way during the quiet moments before Diana's accident.

But that was just crazy. Wishful thinking, at best.

Delusional, at worst. She didn't want to fool herself into believing Dalton cared about her, maybe even loved her, when he so clearly didn't.

Dealing with the grooms got easier when she focused her gaze on their foreheads rather than their lovey-dovey expressions. Before long, the smile she'd plastered on her face began to feel almost genuine. She'd just wrapped a satiny white ribbon around a Drake-blue box containing a cushion-cut diamond solitaire in a platinum setting when the overhead lights flickered and dimmed.

"What's happening?" she asked the salesman as she handed him the box.

"It's closing time." He sighed. "Finally. It's been a day, hasn't it? Thanks for all your help, by the way. What's your name, again?"

Her Royal Highness Princess Aurélie Marchand. "Aurélie."

He nodded. "Thanks again, Aurélie. Good work."

Good work.

No one had ever uttered those words to her before. It gave her a little thrill to be praised for something other than showing up at an event with a tiara on her head. "No problem. Can I do anything else?"

He shrugged. "I've got to close out the registers and get the place cleaned up, then we can all go home."

Home.

Aurélie's throat grew tight. She'd managed to stay so busy for a few hours that she'd forgotten she was supposed to be on a plane right now.

She let out a shaky breath. "I'll help you. I'm not in any hurry."

"Suit yourself," he said and handed her a bottle of Windex and a roll of paper towels.

One by one, the customers left. It was strange being in Drake Diamonds all alone after hours, peaceful in a way that caught Aurélie off guard. After so much noisy activity, there was a grace to the sudden silence. The gemstones almost looked like holy relics glowing in the semi-darkness, the sapphires, rubies and emeralds like precious stained glass.

It was soothing, therapeutic. Almost hypnotic. Aurélie didn't realize how lost she'd become in the simple act of dusting until she heard the salesman's footsteps again.

She gave a start as he walked up behind her. "Sorry. I'm afraid I'm a bit startled."

"As am I."

She froze, unable to move. She could barely even breathe.

That voice.

She knew the particular timbre of that voice. It didn't belong to the salesman. It belonged to the person she wanted to see more than anyone else on earth.

Heart beating wildly in her chest, she turned around. "Dalton."

Chapter Fourteen

Dalton thought he might be hallucinating at first.

He was bone-weary. Diana's accident and its aftermath had exhausted him on every possible level—physically, mentally, emotionally. When he passed through the darkened corridor of Drake Diamonds and glanced toward the Engagements showroom, he didn't think for a second that what he was looking at could possibly be real.

Aurélie was supposed to be on a plane. She couldn't be standing in his store after closing time. Even if she'd ignored his request and stayed in New York, she definitely wouldn't be milling about in Engagements, of all places. When his gaze landed on the dust rag in her right hand, he was sure he was seeing things.

He was wrong of course. But what surprised him even more than Aurélie's presence was the wave of relief that washed over him when she turned around and said his name.

Dalton had never needed anyone before, and that was no accident. He'd arranged his life so that he was self-reliant in every way. He always had been. He didn't want to need anyone or anything.

But right now, he needed *her*. Aurélie. He needed her so badly it terrified him to his core.

He didn't know why she was here. Or how. All he knew was that he felt like falling to his knees in gratitude that she'd ignored him when he'd sent her away.

He shoved his hands in his pockets to stop himself from reaching for her. He couldn't be trusted. Not in the state he was in. If he touched her now, he wouldn't be able to stop. "What are you doing here?"

"I could ask you the same thing." She fiddled with the rag in her hands, nervously wadding it into a ball.

What on earth was going on? It was like he'd stepped into some weird reverse Cinderella scenario.

"I own this building," he said. "I have every right to be here."

"I suppose you do." Her gaze darted toward the empty hallway.

"You can stop looking around. I've sent everyone home already." Almost everyone.

"Oh." She swallowed, and Dalton traced the movement up and down the length of her regal neck. His willpower was crumbling by the second. "How's Diana? Is she going to be okay?"

He nodded. "Yes, thank God. She's awake. Mostly anyway. According to the doctor, she didn't suffer any permanent damage."

He dropped his gaze to the display case and the diamond rings shimmering in the darkness, like ice on fire. "Her horse had to be put down. She didn't know. I told her about an hour ago, and she didn't take it well."

His voice broke, and something inside him seemed to break right along with it. Giving Diana the news about Diamond had been the most difficult conversation he'd ever had in his life. Even more difficult than telling Clarissa's parents about her suicide.

He was just so sick of loss. Of death and dying. He couldn't carry it with him anymore. Not another damned minute.

His gaze slid back to Aurélie, standing in front of him looking so beautiful. So alive. So real.

It was enough to make him lose his head.

"I was engaged once," he said, nodding at the neat row of rings beneath the glass.

What was he doing? He hadn't planned on telling Aurélie about Clarissa. He hadn't even considered it. But once it slipped out, he felt instantly lighter. Just a little bit. Just enough that he could breathe again.

"She died," he continued. "By her own hand, but I was to blame."

He took a deep inhale and paused. He wasn't sure why. Maybe he was waiting for her to respond in horror. Maybe he'd held onto the words for so long that his voice was rebelling. But he forced them out. If he didn't say them now, he knew he never would. To anyone. He'd carry his horrible secrets to his grave, and he couldn't bear the weight of them any longer.

"She called me for help, but I didn't answer. If I had, she might still be alive today." He covered his face with his hands. It hurt to be this open, this vulnerable.

"I should have been there for her, but I wasn't. I was here. Right where I always am." He forced himself to look at Aurélie. As much as he feared seeing a look of disappointment on her face—or worse, pity—he needed to gaze into those glittering green eyes.

The compassion he saw in their emerald depths kept him going. And once he began, he couldn't get the words out fast enough. His tongue tripped over them, and he told her the entire story. He even told her little details he'd thought he'd forgotten, like the shooting star he'd seen on the way home that night and the way he'd felt like the world's biggest fraud when the mourners at Clarissa's funeral offered their condolences. He talked until there was nothing left to say.

Then he finished, breathless, and waited for her to say something. He hoped to God she didn't try and tell him it wasn't his fault. He'd been having that argument with himself for six years. He didn't want to have it with her, too.

She didn't tell him he was blameless, though. She didn't try to make him feel better, nor did she look at him like he was some kind of monster. She said the only thing he was willing to hear. The right thing. The perfect thing.

"Dalton, I'm so sorry." She placed a gentle hand on his forearm.

His name was like a prayer on her lips, her touch like a balm. The tenderness of the moment ripped him open, crushed what was left of his defenses. Without the shelter of his secrets, he was no longer capable of hiding his desperation.

He a*ched* for her.

Keeping his distance from her had been torture. The only thing stopping him from kissing her right here, right now, were those six words he'd been trying to forget since the moment she'd uttered them just hours after he'd taken her to bed.

I don't think it should happen again.

Dalton had never once come close to forcing himself on a woman. He thought men who did that were despicable. He couldn't...wouldn't...kiss her without her consent. But by God, if he stood much longer in that room, drowning in engagement rings, he was liable to do something he'd come to regret. He may already have.

"Princess," he whispered as he reached to cup her face, drawing the pad of his thumb across her lovely lower lip.

She didn't say a word, didn't even breathe as far as he could tell, just gazed at him with her sparkling emerald eyes.

Dalton remembered a story his grandfather had told him when he was a little boy. He'd said that in ancient Rome, the Emperor Nero watched gladiator battles through a large emerald stone because he found the color soothing. Since the very first emerald had been dug out of the ground, people believed healing could be found in their glittering green depths. They were once called the Jewel of Kings.

It was a fitting thing to remember in the presence of royalty.

Dalton could have been Nero in that moment. Soothed and whole. Everything he wanted, everything he needed was right there in those eyes. Acceptance. Life. Passion.

He wanted her. He wanted her again. And again and again.

Walk away.

Walk away while you still can.

"Kiss me." She turned her head just slightly, just

enough for his thumb to make contact with the wet warmth of her mouth. "Please."

Please.

Dalton went rock-hard even before his lips crashed down on hers. Had it only been a day since he'd been inside her? Impossible. It felt like years since he'd buried himself between her thighs and felt her lithe body shuddering beneath him. Too long. Much too long.

He circled an arm around her, pulling her against him as her lips opened for him and he licked his way inside her mouth with teasing strokes of his tongue. He kissed her with all the dark intensity that made him who he was. A shock of pure, primal pleasure shot through him when she whimpered and melted into him.

This, he thought.

This right here was what he wanted. What he'd missed.

She tasted like promise and hunger and hope, things Dalton had given up on long ago. And the way she responded to his touch was enough to bring him back to life.

He pinned her against one of the taller display cases and kissed her until she began to tremble violently. Until the diamonds behind her shook on their glass shelves. He liked it. He liked it far too much.

He wasn't going to rush things this time. Not even if she urged him to hurry. Not even if she begged. Hell, he *wanted* her to beg. He wanted her wet, helpless and desperate for him by the time he pushed inside her. He wanted this to mean something, so when daylight came, it would be impossible for her to look him in the eye and call this a mistake.

"Dalton," she whispered against his mouth. Her hand

moved from his chest to his fly, finding him through his clothes. Exploring. Caressing. Stroking with just the right amount of pressure.

His vision blurred. He groaned. For a moment he thought he saw stars, but then he realized it was the light from the diamonds shimmering softly behind her.

"I want you," she murmured. The next sound he heard was the slide of his zipper, then her delicate hand was around his shaft, pumping slowly. He closed his eyes, lost to the pure, hot bliss of her touch. Only for a moment. Only long enough for his desire to take on an edge of desperation.

He opened his eyes.

"Not now, princess. Not yet." *Not even close.*

He dropped his lips to the curve of her neck and worked his way down, down to the hollow of her throat, casually unbuttoning her dress as he went.

"Turn around," he said in as even a tone as he could manage.

She released her hold on his cock and obeyed, turning slowly, peering at him coyly over her shoulder. But there was heat glimmering in her emerald gaze. Molten desire.

"Put your hands over your head," he told her, his voice raw with need.

Again she did as he said without a moment's hesitation, and that alone was nearly enough to make him lose control. His hands shook as he gathered the soft folds of her dress and lifted it carefully over her head. He tossed it aside, and waves of golden curls spilled over her shoulders and down her supple back.

So gorgeous.

He drank in the sight of her exquisite curves, surrounded by the luminous diamond glow and clothed in

nothing but tiny wisps of lace. She was the most beautiful woman Dalton had ever set eyes on. Always would
be. He couldn't say how, or why, but he knew with abso-
lute certainty that there would never be another woman
in his life like Aurélie. Whatever this was between them
came around only once in a lifetime. If that.

"Be still," he said. "Be very still."

Her hair rippled gently beneath his breath. He twirled
a long, lovely lock of it around his fingertips before trail-
ing his hand ever so softly down the length of his spine.
His touch left goose bumps in its wake.

She shivered.

He leaned in, pressed a tender kiss between her shoulder blades, and a slow smile of satisfaction came to his
lips when she arched her back.

So needy.

Now we're getting somewhere.

What was he doing to her?

This wasn't like before. This was something different entirely. Something far more intense.

He'd been holding back last night. She realized that
now. She'd asked him not to be gentle, not to go slow.
And he hadn't. But tonight, Dalton was the one in control. He was setting the pace. And the deliberate slow-
ness of his movements seemed designed to send her into
sensual distress.

Aurélie could barely keep herself upright. Her legs
were on the verge of buckling, and Dalton had barely
touched her. There'd been just a few brushes of his fingertips and one or two lingering kisses, but it was the
wicked edge to his voice that was reducing her to a quivering mass of need. He sounded so serious. So imposing.

It shouldn't have aroused her. It absolutely shouldn't have, but it did. It inflamed her in a way she didn't understand. Couldn't, even if she'd been capable of trying. Which she wasn't. Not by a long shot.

She couldn't think. She couldn't speak. When he ran his hands down her sides, grabbed hold of her hips and gently turned her around so she was facing him again, she could barely even look at him.

She peered up at him through the thick fringe of her lashes and her face went hot. His lips curved into a knowing grin as she struggled to catch her breath. She glanced down. Her breasts were straining the lacy cups of her bra, arching toward him. Her thighs were pressed together in an effort to quell the tingling at her center. This was too much. Too much heat. Too much sensation. It didn't matter that she couldn't speak. She didn't need to say a word. Her body was pleading with him, begging him to touch her. Take her. Fill her.

She would have been mortified if she hadn't been so violently aroused.

He raised a single, dark eyebrow and pushed the hair back from her eyes. Her pulse rocketed out of control, and his gaze dropped to her throat. He knew. Dalton Drake knew perfectly well what he was doing to her.

She licked her lips and willed herself not to beg. *Please, Dalton. Touch me.*

Love me.

Love me.

At last he moved closer, unhooked her bra and slid its satiny straps down her arms. Before it even fell to the floor, his mouth was on her breasts, licking, sucking, biting. Then he pressed a languid, openmouthed kiss to her belly. She was vaguely conscious of her panties sliding down her legs. Everything had gone so seductively fuzzy around the edges. She looked around, and she saw Dalton's image reflected in the cool facets of the diamonds twinkling under the shimmering lights. Everywhere. Like a starry winter's night.

Her legs trembled as he parted her thighs, his mouth moving lower, lower still.

The scrape of his five o'clock shadow along the soft flesh of her inner thigh was nearly enough to send her over the edge. What was happening? This was too intimate. Too intense. There would be no coming back from this. She'd never be able to pretend this didn't matter. Not to herself. Not to him.

He'd told her his deepest, darkest secret. And now he was uncovering hers, exposing her desire for the wanton, yearning thing that it was. She couldn't be this vulnerable to him. Not when she would eventually have to walk away.

She'd stolen another day. But this wouldn't last forever. It couldn't. She'd be lucky if it lasted until the gala.

The impossibility of the situation bore down on her. She looked at Dalton settled between her thighs, pleasuring her with his skillful mouth and she felt like crying. But instead she heard herself crying out in pleasure, saying his name as though she had a right to it. As though it belonged to her.

He's not yours.

He's not yours, and he never will be.

"Dalton," she murmured. She had to tell him. He'd been so honest with her. So real. And he still didn't know why she'd been so desperate to leave home.

"Let go." There it was again—that unflinchingly authoritative tone. Her favorite sound. "Just feel, princess."

Surrender was her only choice. It was too late for anything else. She clung tightly to him, her hands moving through his hair as she writhed against him.

Just feel, princess.

Her head fell back as she fully, finally gave herself up to him. She couldn't fight it anymore. It was no use. He slipped a finger inside her, moving it in time with his mouth. She gasped, blinking in shock at the astonishing pleasure. Her mind had caught up with her body, stripped bare and open. Everything around her shimmered. Her eyes fluttered shut, and the row of dazzling engagement rings in the case beside her was the last thing she saw before her climax slammed into her and she came apart.

Dalton caught her as she slipped toward the floor. He tucked an arm beneath her legs and carried her out of the room, down the hall to his office. She tried to wrap her arms around his neck, but they'd gone impossibly heavy. Instead she nestled her head in the warm space between his neck and shoulder.

He set her down gingerly on the sofa and undressed while she watched, memorizing every detail of his sculpted body and the way it glistened like fine marble in the moonlight streaming through the window. She wanted to hold onto what she was feeling right then—the heady thrill she felt when he looked at her bare body.

He sees me.

He always has.

He stretched out next to her, and she moved to sit astride him. She gazed down at him, this man who'd found her when she hadn't even realized how lost she'd been. He rose up to kiss her, his mouth gentle and seeking. It was a reverent kiss. Worshipful, almost. The tenderness of it caught her off guard. A wistful ache squeezed her heart.

She reached for him and guided him to her entrance. She needed him to fill her again. Now, before whatever was happening between them slipped through their fingers like her mother's golden pearls.

With an excruciatingly sweet ache, he pushed inside her. Slowly, slowly, and she arched to take him in. He curled his strong hands around her hips, thrust harder. And harder. Until the sweetness gave way to blazing heat, and fire bloomed between them once again.

Diamond bright.

Chapter Fifteen

Dalton slept like the dead.

With Aurélie's head on his chest and his fingers buried in her hair, he slept the peaceful, dreamless slumber of a man who'd managed to outrun his demons. His eyes didn't open a fraction until he heard voices. Familiar voices.

"Good morning."

"I understand. There's been a family emergency, but the moment I'm able to reach Mr. Drake, I'll let him know you're here."

Was that Mrs. Barnes? What was his secretary doing in his apartment?

He pressed his eyes closed, determined not to care. He wasn't waking up. Not yet. He wanted to stay right where he was, wrapped in Aurélie's graceful limbs as long as he could. He turned, slid behind her and burrowed into her soft orchid scent. Memories from the night before came flooding back. Tastes. Sounds. The glorious sight of her sitting on top of him with her hair tumbling over her shoulders and moonlight caressing her beautiful breasts. He ran his hands over the soft swell of her hips, pulled her close to grind against her bottom and was rewarded with a sultry moan.

"Good morning, love," he whispered, already hard, already wanting her. God, what was happening to him? He was insatiable.

"I understand the urgency of the situation, but it's really not best that you come here, Your Highness."

Somewhere beneath the liquid heat of his arousal, a prickle of unease snaked its way into Dalton's consciousness.

His eyes drifted open, and he took in his surroundings. His desk. His chair. The Drake-blue walls.

Shit. They weren't in his apartment. They were in his office.

"Aurélie, wake up. We've overslept." Sunlight and the crystal reflection of snowfall streamed through his office windows.

What time was it? He never slept past 6 a.m. From the looks of things, it was far later than that. And if Mrs. Barnes was already here...

He cursed and jerked upright. The store was about to open for business. The hallways were teeming with his employees. And he was naked in his office.

With Aurélie.

She blinked, then as the reality of the present circumstances dawned, her eyes went wide with panic. "Dalton. Oh my God."

"Don't worry." He glanced at the halfway open door,

leaped off the sofa and slammed it closed. "Everything will be okay."

Her gaze darted around the room. "But my clothes…"

Shit. Shit. Shit. Her dress was still pooled on the floor of Engagements, right next to her lingerie. Not to mention the fact that there were cameras all over that room. He needed to get his hands on the store's surveillance videos. Immediately, before anyone saw them. But first he needed to get her dressed.

He laid his hands on her shoulders and pressed a kiss to the top of her head. *Don't panic.* "It will be fine. I promise. I'll go get your clothes."

She nodded, looking every bit as dazed as he felt.

How had he let this happen? He'd had sex in the store. Even Artem had never done something this outrageous. That Dalton knew of.

He shook his head. If this wasn't the first time a Drake had been in this situation, he really didn't want to know.

He grabbed his pants from the floor and pulled them on. They were wrinkled as hell. Everyone in the building would be able to recognize his stroll through the store as a walk of shame. Marvelous.

At least he had a selection of pressed shirts from the dry cleaners in one of his desk drawers. He reached for the one on top of the stack and pulled it on, fumbling with the buttons.

"Let me," Aurélie said, unfolding her legs from beneath her and walking toward him.

He allowed himself a brief glance of her bare body, even though he knew good and well it would only make him forget why he was in such a hurry to leave the room. Sure enough, one look, one glimpse of her porcelain skin, her perfect breasts and their rosebud nipples, was all it took for him to forget about everything on the other side of the door.

"Stop looking at me like that, or we'll never get out of here." She rolled her eyes and smoothed down his collar.

He felt himself grinning. "Would that be so bad?"

"You tell me, Mr. CEO."

"It might be a tad inappropriate." His hands found her waist and slid lower until they cupped the decadent softness of her bottom. "Not that I care much at the moment."

She smiled up at him and something came unloose in his chest. "But you will. Eventually."

He was beginning to doubt it.

"There. You're all buttoned up."

A pity. "How do I look?"

"Like you've been ravaging women on the sales floor." She lifted an amused brow.

"*Woman,* not *women.*" He slid his arms around her, not quite willing to tear himself away despite the absurdity of the situation. "Only the one."

The one.

The One.

"Good to know, Mr. Drake." She rose up on tiptoe and kissed the corner of his mouth, and for a moment his feet stayed rooted to the floor. He couldn't have budged for all the diamonds in Africa.

The intercom on his office phone buzzed, piercing the intimate silence. "Dalton, it's Artem. If you're in there, we need to talk. It's urgent."

He took his hands off Aurélie. Came to his senses.

"I'll be right back," he said.

Artem was waiting for him directly on the other side

of the door, holding Aurélie's clothes and wearing a grim expression.

Perfect. Just perfect.

"Whatever you're going to say, I really don't want to hear it right now. Can we talk later?"

Artem thrust Aurélie's things at him. "No, it can't."

"Fine. Lecture me all you want." God knows, he deserved it.

Artem lowered his voice. "Brother, I'm not here to lecture you. Believe me. We've got a situation on our hands."

"It's not Diana, is it?" That couldn't be it, though, could it? Otherwise, Artem wouldn't be here.

"No, she's fine. I just spoke to her doctor this morning." He sighed. "It's the palace. They've been calling. And calling. Mrs. Barnes is in a panic. Have you checked your messages?"

Dalton's gut churned. After Diana's fall, he'd forgotten all about the unread email. He hadn't even turned his phone back on.

He shook his head. "Is this as bad as it seems?"

"It's not good." Artem raked a hand through his hair. He seemed to be doing everything in his power to remain calm. "Get her dressed, and we'll deal with it. Together. Sound good?"

He nodded. "Thanks."

"That's what family's for." But there was a gravity in his expression that Dalton couldn't ignore.

"Wait. What aren't you telling me?"

Artem shook his head. His gaze dropped to the floor, and Dalton suddenly didn't want to know. He just wanted to rewind the clock to the night before and stay in that dazzling place forever.

"She's engaged." Artem sighed. "Aurélie. She's getting married. It's on the front page of every newspaper in the world."

Dalton shook his head.

There had to be some kind of mistake. He was talking about some other princess. Not her. Not Aurélie.

The one.

The One.

He swallowed hard. "No." Just...no.

She would have said something. She would have told him, wouldn't she?

A dark fury began to gather in his chest, like a rising storm. So thick, so black he choked it on it. He cleared his throat, swallowed it down, as he remembered how lost she'd been when she first arrived in New York, how she'd pushed him away after the first time they'd made love...how she'd hated even setting foot in Engagements. She *had* told him, hadn't she? Not in so many words, but he'd known. On some level, he'd known. She'd been telling him all along.

Artem reached into the inside pocket of his suit jacket and pulled out a neatly folded square of newsprint. "Here. Read it for yourself."

He didn't want to look. He really didn't. But he forced himself to unfold the paper, because he'd been blind enough for the past few days. It was time to wake up to reality.

Her Royal Highness Princess Aurélie Marchand of Delamotte to Marry Duke Lawrence Bouvier on April 20 in Lavish Royal Wedding

* * *

Aurélie knew something was horribly wrong as soon as Dalton crossed the threshold.

There was a sudden seriousness in the firm set of his jaw, and he seemed to look right through her when he handed her the folded pile of clothes. Suddenly acutely aware of her nakedness, she wanted to hide. If anything, to shield herself from the coolness in his gaze.

"Thank you," she said and slipped into her dress as quickly as she could.

He said nothing, just stood there waiting with a large Drake-blue shopping bag in his hands while she pulled on her panties.

What was going on? What had happened in the handful of minutes since she'd seen him last?

She swallowed and smoothed down the front of her dress. She knew, even without the benefit of a mirror, that she looked like a mess. A complete and utter disaster. "Dalton, what's wrong?"

"Nothing's wrong." He shrugged with a casual air of nonchalance, but the impassivity of his gaze shifted into something darker. More dangerous. "I should probably offer my congratulations, though."

For a moment, she was confused. She couldn't imagine what he was talking about.

Then she realized…

Somehow he'd found out about the wedding. He *knew*.

No. He couldn't. That wasn't feasible. How could he possibly know when it wasn't even official?

"I'm not sure I know what you mean." But her words sounded disingenuous, even to her own ears.

She hated herself.

"Save it, Princess," he snapped.

With exaggerated calmness, he pulled a newspaper from the top of the shopping bag and handed it to her.

She was afraid to take it, but she didn't dare refuse him. Not when she'd already given him every reason in the world to despise her.

Her stomach plummeted when she read the headline. The palace had made an announcement. Without even consulting her. Without her knowledge. She supposed it didn't matter after all that she'd been a no-show for the sitting with Lord Clement. They'd simply used an older picture.

She stared at herself, smiling like an idiot below the awful headline, and realized that her absence *had* mattered. It mattered so much that the palace had gone ahead and released the news. They'd played the ultimate trump card. She had no choice but to go home now. She'd never be able to move about New York, or anyplace else now, without being recognized. Not after this.

She folded the newspaper and dropped it on Dalton's desk. She couldn't stand to look at it another minute. If she did, she might vomit.

"Dalton, please. Let me explain. I wasn't engaged when I came here. I'm not..."

But she was.

She knew it. And so did he. So did everyone. She was getting married, and it was front-page news.

Someone knocked on the door, and Aurélie wished with everything in her that Dalton would tell whomever it was to go away. She needed to talk to him. She needed to fix things. She didn't know how it was possible, but she had to try. She'd never be able to live with herself if she didn't.

"Come in," he said.

The door opened, and in walked Mrs. Barnes, followed by an older gentleman wearing a dark suit and a grim expression. Aurélie's father.

Her legs gave way, and she sank onto the sofa. Her father had come all this way, just to drag her home. It was over—her holiday, Dalton, their bargain.

All of it.

"I'm sorry, Mr. Drake." Mrs. Barnes was wringing her hands, and fluttering about between Dalton and her father. "I apologize, but Mr. Marchand insisted on seeing you. I know he doesn't have an appointment…"

Dalton held up a hand. "It's okay. He doesn't need one."

Of course he didn't. The Crown Prince of Delamotte always got his way.

Bile rose to the back of Aurélie's throat.

"Father," she said.

"Aurélie." He looked her up and down, from the messy hair atop her head to the tips of her barefoot toes. Her face burned with shame. Her father didn't say a word about the meaning of her disheveled appearance. He didn't have to. He swiveled his gaze toward Dalton. "Mr. Drake, I presume?"

"Yes." Dalton nodded. The fact that he refused to bow was a major breach of royal etiquette. Aurélie suspected he knew this. She also suspected he didn't give a damn.

"My office has been trying to reach you, Mr. Drake. Aurélie failed to show up for an important engagement yesterday, so we tracked her cell phone." His lips straightened into a flat line. "Imagine my surprise when it was brought to my attention that she's been here in New York. For days, it seems."

They must have tracked her phone before she'd taken out the SIM card. They'd known where she was all along.

The air in the room went so thick that Aurélie couldn't seem to catch her breath. Her father was giving Dalton a warning. He didn't care if Dalton was her lover. He was nothing to the Crown Prince of Delamotte. No one.

Dalton shrugged. "Forgive me, Your Highness, but your daughter is a grown woman. I believe she can make her own decisions."

He glanced at her, but she couldn't even look at him. This was so much worse than anything she'd ever imagined taking place. What had she done?

"Aurélie," Dalton prompted.

If ever there was a time to stand up to her father, it was now.

She took a deep breath and met his gaze, but when she did, she didn't see the man who'd bounced her on his knee when she was a little girl. She saw her sovereign. She saw the crown. She saw everything her mother had written on the gilt-edged pages of her diary about the tragedy of fate.

"I don't want to go, and I can't marry the duke." The words came out far weaker than she'd intended.

"Nonsense. You can, and you will. I won't allow you to embarrass me, Aurélie. Nor the throne." Her father glanced at his watch. "Come along. We can discuss this when we get home. We have a plane to catch."

She shook her head. "But my things…" Her dog. Her mother's pearls. *Her heart.*

If Dalton hadn't stepped forward and handed her the shopping bag, she may have found the strength to stay. She liked to believe that she would have been able to make that choice, that she would have been strong

enough to stand up for what she wanted. Love. Life.
Freedom. But when she looked down and saw what Dalton was offering her, she lost her resolve.

At the bottom of the bag sat a black velvet box, embossed with the Marchand royal crest. She knew what was inside without opening it. It was the secret egg. He was giving it back to her. He wanted her gone, no matter the cost.

"I've made arrangements for Sam to deliver Jacques and the rest of your things to the airport," Dalton said coolly. He nodded at the bag.

Take it from him. Just take it.

She dug deep and summoned her pride. If he didn't want her, she wouldn't stay. He'd already sent her away once. Twice was more than she could take.

She lifted her chin and reached for the bag. Only then did she notice the small glass box on top of the velvet egg carrier. Inside were her mother's gold pearls, restrung and perfect.

Just as perfect as she was expected to be from now on.

Chapter Sixteen

Dalton operated on autopilot until the night of the gala. Those seven days were the longest of his life. He spent all day, every day at the office, preparing for the party. He talked to the caterer, the florist, the baker and the linen rental company. He gave press interviews. More press interviews than he'd ever conducted before. He didn't particularly enjoy talking about the Marchand family over and over again. But he was determined not to let it show.

He spent his evenings at the hospital, sitting at Diana's bedside, until she was discharged. After Dr. Larson released her, Dalton insisted she come stay at his apartment so he could keep an eye on her. He worried about her. He didn't like the thought of her grieving for Diamond alone, in her tiny Brooklyn walk-up. At least that was what he'd told Diana. And the rest of the Drakes.

And himself.

The truth of the matter was that he was the one who couldn't handle the solitude of an empty apartment. Everywhere he turned, he saw reminders of Aurélie: Central Park, the New York Public Library, the sidewalk outside of Bergdorf Goodman. His office. His apartment. His bed.

God, how he missed her.

He missed her quirky clothes. He missed the way she never once allowed him to tell her what to do. He even missed her snoring, silly-looking dog. The enormity of her absence may not have fully hit him until one afternoon when he and Diana were walking through the park and he stopped beneath the blue awning at the pet adoption stand.

"Um, what are you doing?" Diana asked, crossing her arms and gaping at him in disbelief as he scooped a scrawny Chihuahua from one of the pens.

Was he going crazy, or had those been his exact words to Aurélie when he'd found her standing in the same spot on the day she'd first arrived?

We're adopting a dog, darling.

"I remember you." The animal shelter volunteer narrowed her gaze at him. She was the same woman from before, wielding her clipboard in the same annoying manner. "You're the one who adopted the little French bulldog."

"The *what?*" Diana let out an astonished laugh. "You have a dog? Where is it?"

The pet adoption counselor stared daggers at him. "You've re-homed the dog? You can't do that, sir. You signed an agreement."

"I didn't re-home the dog. Look, this is all just a misunderstanding. I assure you."

But even the Chihuahua seemed to be giving him the evil eye.

Marvelous.

He set the little dog back down in its tiny playpen and moved on before he got arrested for dognapping or something equally ridiculous.

He and Diana walked the length of the park in silence. They passed the zoo, and the roar of the lions sounded strangely lonely in the snowfall. Then they made their way down the Literary Walk, and when they had to dodge out of the way to avoid a dog walker and her tangle of half a dozen leashes, Diana finally said something.

"Are you going to tell me about the missing dog? Because the suspense is killing me." She stopped in front of the statue of William Shakespeare.

The Bard peered at Dalton over her shoulder, looking every bit as serious and judgmental as the pet adoption counselor. *Or maybe I really am losing my mind.*

He sighed. "There's nothing to tell. The dog didn't belong to me. Aurélie adopted him, and she took him with her when she left. End of story. Can we keep walking now? The gala is tonight, and I've got things to do."

"No, we can't just keep walking and pretend nothing is going on." She shook her head and brushed back a loose strand of hair that had escaped from her hat.

She looked good. Healthy. But she still had a definite air of sadness about her. Dalton wished she'd start riding again, but he supposed getting back on a horse would just take time.

She crossed her arms. "You're in love with her, aren't you? You *love* her, and you miss her. That's why you wanted me to move into your apartment. That's why you were just mooning over a Chihuahua, isn't it?"

Yes. Yes, God help me. That's exactly why. "No. Don't be ridiculous. You gave us all a scare. I'm your brother, and I want to keep an eye on you. And the dog has nothing to do with Aurélie. Who wouldn't fall for that tiny little face?"

She rolled her eyes. "You're not fooling me, brother dear. You hate dogs."

Used to. He used to hate dogs. It seemed he'd developed a soft spot for them lately. But that was beside the point, especially since it looked as though the animal rescue community had probably blackballed him now.

"Anyway, don't try to change the subject. This isn't about the dog. It's about you." Diana jabbed her pointer finger into Dalton's chest. "And Aurélie."

It hurt to hear her name almost as much as it hurt to say it. "Drop it, Diana. There's nothing to discuss. She's getting married, remember?"

"But she's not." Diana shook her head.

"Yes, she is. On April 20. To a duke or a king or something like that. She'll be wearing a crown on her head, and she'll probably arrive in a damned glass coach."

"Stop yelling."

"I'm not yelling." A passerby pushing a baby carriage gave him an odd look.

Maybe he was yelling. Just a little bit.

"Calm down and listen to me for two seconds, would you? She's not getting married. I read it in the paper this morning."

"How many times have I told you that you can't believe everything you read in *Page Six*?" Artem had only actually participated in half the debauchery he'd been accused of in that rag. At least that was what he'd insisted at the time.

"Sheesh, give me some credit. I didn't read it in *Page*

Six. It was on the front page of the Books section of the *New York Times*."

He paused for a second and glanced at William Shakespeare while he tried to absorb what his sister was saying. He thought of star-crossed lovers and fate and destiny. Then he remembered how that particular story ended.

"You're mistaken," he said flatly. The one thing he wanted less than pity was false hope. "Why would news about a royal wedding appear in the Books section?"

She lifted a knowing brow. "You know what? I'm not going to tell you. You're going to have to read it for yourself."

"Diana." He meant it as a warning, but despite himself, the faintest glimmer of hope stirred in his chest.

Stop. It's over. She's not even in the country anymore.

"This is what you get for only looking at the Business section of the *Times*, by the way. There's a whole world out there that you know nothing about."

"Thank you for the sisterly advice," he said wryly.

"You're welcome, my dear brother." She rubbed her mitten-covered hands together and looped an arm through his. "Shall we walk home now? It's freezing out, and like you said, we need to get ready for your big gala."

Clearly she wasn't going to tell him anything else. And suddenly the gala seemed like the furthest thing from Dalton's mind. "Fine."

"There's a newsstand on the corner of Central Park South and 50th Street, you know. We'll pass right by it on the way home."

"Indeed. I know." He'd already made a mental note of that very fact. It was the same newsstand where he picked up his paper nearly every morning. Not that his nosy sister needed to know any more about his personal life.

He managed to grab a copy of the *Times*, pay for it and walk the rest of the way home without tearing it open and poring over the Books section. He wanted to do so in private, even though the cat was already apparently out of the bag and Diana knew how much Aurélie meant to him. Now that the possibility that she might not be going through with the wedding had been dangled in front of him, he was consumed by the idea.

He didn't see how it was possible, yet with everything in him, he wanted to believe. He wanted to believe so badly that when he'd finally closed himself off in the privacy of his bedroom, he was almost afraid to spread the newspaper open on his bed.

He tossed it down beside his Armani tuxedo and Drake-blue bowtie and told himself if Diana had been wrong, or if she'd simply been playing some cruel joke on him, nothing would change. He didn't need Aurélie in his life. He hadn't crumbled to pieces after she'd left. He was a Drake. He was perfectly content.

Liar.

He poured himself a glass of scotch, took a generous gulp and finally sat down on the edge of the bed. His hands were shaking, and the paper rattled as he tossed aside the front page and the Business section. Then there it was, emblazoned across the header of the Books section.

Her Royal Highness Aurélie Marchand
of Delamotte Calls Off Wedding Following
Announcement of New Book Deal

Oh my God.

Diana was right.

He read the headline three times to make sure he wasn't seeing things. Then he dove into the article, which said that Aurélie had sold the publishing rights to her mother's diary. Due to overwhelming public interest in the book, the publication of the diary had been fast-tracked. It was due to hit shelves on April 20, what would have been Aurélie's wedding day.

Dalton sat very still and tried to absorb the implications of what he'd just read. There was much the article didn't say. Was Aurélie staying in Delamotte? How had her father reacted to this extreme act of defiance? Would she be stripped of her crown?

Does she still love me?

Did she ever?

He told himself what he'd just read had no bearing on his life whatsoever. It was about Aurélie taking control of *her* life.

Not about him.

Not about them.

But damned if it didn't feel like a second chance.

Dalton folded the newspaper and slowly sipped the rest of his scotch. He dressed for the gala with the utmost care, slipping into his waistcoat and fastening his Drake Diamond cufflinks. He caught a glimpse of himself in his bedroom mirror as he reached for his tie and paused, marveling at how composed he appeared on the outside when he couldn't seem to stop the violent pounding of his heart.

He stared down at the Drake-blue tie in his hand and realized he couldn't put it on. *This is where the charade stops,* he thought. *This is where it ends.*

If Aurélie could choose, then so could he.

Thirty minutes later, he barged into Artem's office without bothering to knock. "I need to talk to you."

He'd walked straight through the first floor showroom without even a cursory glance at the display cases that housed the Marchand eggs. He should be overseeing the arrangement of the collection. The Drake Diamonds staff had strict instructions that Dalton was to have final approval before the doors opened for the gala. But he and Diana had only just arrived and what he had to say to Artem couldn't wait.

"Perfect. Because there's something I need to tell you before the gala begins." Artem glanced at his watch. "Which is in just fifteen minutes, so I may as well come out and say it."

Dalton shook his head. If he didn't do this now, he might never actually get the words out. "I'd really rather go first."

Artem raked a hand through his hair and sighed. "But…"

"I quit," Dalton blurted at the exact same moment that Artem leveled his gaze and said, "You're fired."

The brothers stared at each other for a beat, shocked into silence.

Finally, Artem cleared his throat. "Well this works out rather nicely, don't you think?"

"Wait a minute." Dalton sank into the leather chair opposite Artem. "You can't fire me. You don't have the authority. We're co-CEOs, remember?"

He didn't even know why he was arguing about it when the bottom line was the same—he was finished at Drake Diamonds. He'd had enough. If Aurélie could be brave enough to take hold of her future and change it, then so could he.

Except that he'd never been fired from a job in his life. And he also owned one third of the family business.

"Yes and no." Artem shrugged. "We agreed to share the position, but never drew up paperwork to make the change official."

"It was a gentleman's agreement." How could Dalton have anticipated the need for paperwork? Artem had always been the one constantly threatening to turn in his resignation.

My, how things change.

"Exactly." Artem shrugged and brushed an invisible speck of lint from the shoulder of his tuxedo jacket. When had he gotten so casually adept at running the company? Dalton had nothing to worry about. Drake Diamonds would be in safe hands. "As far as the paperwork goes, I'm the sole CEO of Drake Diamonds, which means…"

"You can fire me." Dalton smiled. Who smiled as he was being fired? By his own brother, no less?

I do, apparently.

"Right." Artem tilted his head and slid his hands into his pocket as he examined Dalton. "And might I say, you're taking it awfully well."

It was Dalton's turn to shrug. "That's because I quit, effective the moment this gala is over."

"You're still fired. Don't take it personally, but you can't be trusted to stay away. You've done an excellent job here. You've poured everything you have into Drake Diamonds, but it's time for you to get an actual life." He had the decency to wince, but only for a second. "No offense, of course."

"None taken." Dalton rolled his eyes.

"Come on, you know I'm right. If Diana's accident taught us anything, it's that life is precious."

Exactly.

Except Dalton should have learned that lesson years ago. Six years ago, to be exact.

How had he allowed himself to waste so much time? So much life? Aside from Diana's accident, the handful of days he'd spent with Aurélie had been the best he'd ever experienced. But he hadn't fully appreciated them, had he? Save for the times they'd made love, he'd held her at arm's length. It was time to hold her close. Now and forever.

If she'd still let him.

"Yes, you're right. That's why I'm leaving for Delamotte first thing in the morning. Or tonight, if I can arrange a flight." He had no idea how he'd even get an audience with a royal princess. But he'd figure it out. He'd kick down the palace doors if necessary.

"I'd hoped Her Royal Highness might have something to do with your decision." Artem's face split into a huge grin. "Let me be the first to congratulate you."

Dalton shook his head. "Not so fast. I don't even know if she's still speaking to me."

He'd sent her packing. Twice. That was a lot to atone for.

"I see." Artem nodded and glanced at his watch. "As much as I'd like to give you a brotherly pep talk right about now, there's no time. You should probably go take a look at the eggs and make sure everything is in order, no?"

"Will do." Dalton rose to his feet, buttoned the jacket of his tux and turned to go.

He was nearly out the door when he heard Artem say, "Nice tie, by the way."

Dalton just shook his head, laughed and headed for the elevator.

The first floor was abuzz with activity. Every member of the Drake Diamonds staff was on hand. Through the glass revolving door, he could see photographers and other members of the press lined up on the snowy sidewalk, waiting for the official start of the unveiling.

Excellent. After the many professional mistakes he'd made over the course of the past month, it was comforting to know he was leaving on a successful note.

Except as he approached the exhibit and spotted the Marchand jeweled hen egg in the first glass case, he sighed. Something wasn't right. The hen egg was the oldest piece in the collection. It had been the egg featured on all the banners and advertisements. Dalton had left instructions for it to be placed in the center of the room, in the illuminated glass case that had once housed the revered Drake Diamond.

Someone had screwed up.

He really didn't need this now. Not when the gala was set to begin in less than five minutes, and not when he had far more important things on his mind. Like how to woo a princess.

"Excuse me." He beckoned the closest employee he could find. "Who arranged the eggs this way?"

"Your brother did, sir." The salesman gestured overhead, toward the upper floors of the building. "We followed the exhibit map you'd drawn up, but Mr. Drake came down about half an hour ago and changed everything."

Dalton's fists clenched at his sides. What the hell was

going on with Artem? Firing him after he quit was one thing. Completely usurping him before he was even gone was another matter entirely.

The salesman shifted uneasily from one foot to the other. Clearly he wasn't thrilled to be the bearer of such news. Not that Dalton could blame him. "He said you might be upset, and he indicated if you wanted to discuss it, you should go upstairs to Engagements."

"Engagements?" Had his brother had an aneurysm or something? They weren't even opening Engagements up to customers tonight. Everyone was to stay on the first floor.

The salesman cleared his throat. "But first he said you should take a look at the exhibit's centerpiece, Mr. Drake."

The centerpiece.

He'd been so thrown by the obviously incorrect placement of the jeweled hen egg that he hadn't even ventured a glance at the big case in the center. Who knew what Artem had stuck in there?

He turned, and what he saw stole the breath from his lungs.

On a pedestal in the center of the room, in the very heart of Drake Diamonds, sat a pink-enameled egg, covered in shimmering pavé diamonds and tiny seed pearls.

The Marchand secret egg had found its way back to New York.

Is this a mistake?

The question had followed Aurélie all the way across the Atlantic Ocean. It nagged at her for the duration of the twelve-hour flight, as she sat sleepless in First Class, clutching the black velvet egg box like a security blanket while Jacques snored in his carrier.

Would Dalton be happy to see her? Had he thought about her at all over the past seven days?

God, she hoped so.

She'd thought of little else but him. At night when she closed her eyes, she dreamt of his sighs of pleasure as he'd touched her, kissed her…loved her. When she woke in the morning, his name was the first word on her lips, the memory of him the first tug in her heart.

She'd prayed for it to stop. She'd pleaded with God to make the memories fade.

They hadn't.

If anything, her feelings for Dalton had only grown stronger. No matter what happened now, though, she was grateful for the persistence of memory. She knew that now. Knowing Dalton had changed her. Permanently. Profoundly. If she'd never met him, never fallen in love, she would have never had the courage to stand up to her father. She would have never done what she had to do in order to take control of her own destiny.

She'd paved the way for her own future. All because of him. Because of Dalton Drake.

So even if coming back to New York turned out to be a mistake, even if he took one look at her and told her to go back home, she wouldn't regret a thing.

But she hoped it wasn't a mistake. She hoped he loved her even a tiny fraction as much as she loved him.

The elevator dinged, and her knees grew weak. Jacques yipped in her arms.

This is it.

The doors swished open, and there he was. Aurélie had to bite her lip to keep herself from crying with relief at the sight of him. He looked so handsome. Even more handsome than she remembered. His exquisitely tailored tuxedo showed off his broad shoulders to perfection. Formal wear suited him.

There was just a hint of stubble on his jawline, and his eyes were even steelier than she remembered. They glittered like black diamonds as his gaze swept over her.

Aurélie's breath caught in her throat. She felt like she might faint. Jacques squirmed with such enthusiasm at the sight of Dalton that she had to set him down on the floor. The little dog bounded toward Dalton as if he hadn't seen him in a century. Aurélie wished she could do the same, but she couldn't bring herself to go to him.

Why was this so difficult? She hadn't even been this nervous when she'd finally confronted her father and told him she'd sent her mother's diary to the biggest publisher in Europe. Sad, yes. But nervous, no. Handing over her mother's diary had been bittersweet. She hated to hurt her father, but after the way he'd treated her in New York, he'd left her no choice. It was the only way she could buy her freedom.

It was what her mother would have wanted.

She leaned against one of the glass cases of diamond rings and willed herself to stay upright. But as Dalton scooped Jacques into his arms and moved toward her in the darkness, she noticed something that gave her a tiny glimmer of hope.

Is that...

No, it can't be.

Her gaze locked on the bowtie around Dalton's neck. She couldn't believe what she was seeing. The tie was red. Not Drake-blue, but *red*. Brilliant, blazing red. She couldn't seem to stop staring at it as he made his way toward her.

"Do my eyes deceive me, or is there a princess standing in front of me?" He stood about a foot and a half away. Just out of arm's reach, but close enough to see a hint of the dimple in his left cheek that only seemed to make an appearance on the rare occasions when he laughed.

Aurélie lifted an amused brow. "Is that a red tie, or am I hallucinating?"

"Touché." A smile tugged at his lips, and swarms of butterflies took flight in Aurélie's tummy. Then as quickly as the smile appeared, it was gone. In its place was an ardent expression she couldn't quite decipher. "You brought the egg back."

"You noticed."

"Indeed." He set Jacques down and took a step closer. Aurélie felt herself leaning toward Dalton, as if even gravity couldn't keep them apart. "You didn't need to do that, you know."

"But I did. We had a bargain, remember?" She needed to touch him. She needed to feel him again. It felt like a century had passed since he'd devoured her in this very room.

But her body remembered. She felt divinely liquid just standing in front of him, steeped in memories and decadent sensation. He'd loved her in this room, between these hallowed walls. He'd shared his deepest secrets. He'd done things to her that made the diamonds blush.

"You don't owe me a thing. Our bargain fell apart." He swallowed, and a rather fascinating knot flexed in his chiseled jaw. "That was my fault, Aurélie. I'm sorry."

"Don't. Please." She shook her head and realized too late that she'd started to cry.

She didn't want tears. Not now. She just wanted to throw herself into his arms and end the aching torture of being so close to him without feeling the warmth of his skin beneath her fingertips. She just wanted to kiss him again. And again.

"I..."

But he didn't let her finish. Before she could say a word about ending her engagement, his hands were in her hair, tipping her head back so that his lips were angled perfectly over hers.

"My perfect, precious pearl," he whispered. "Don't cry."

At last he kissed her, gently at first. Then as a tumultuous heat gathered in her center, the kiss grew deeper until she trembled with need. *Please. Please.* He groaned in response to her silent plea and pulled her closer. She could feel every inch of him through the lilac chiffon of her evening gown.

He pulled back slightly, his gaze fixed on her with a new intensity. "Tell me it's true. Tell me you're not marrying him."

"It's true." She nodded, dizzy with desire. Drunk with it. It was frightening how much she wanted him, needed him. She was finished with trying to protect her heart from getting hurt. She'd tried it already and had made a spectacular mess of things. She was all in now. No fear. No regrets.

"The thought of you with another man nearly killed me, princess. Have you come back to stay?" he asked, his voice rough. Questions shone in his diamond eyes.

It was time for answers. Past time.

Her heart pounded wildly. *Do it. Do it now. Say what you came here to say.* "I can't stay. I'm just here for the gala."

Dalton nodded, and the light in his eyes dimmed. "I understand."

For a fraction of a second, the silence between them expanded, threatening to choke them both. Jacques whimpered at their feet.

"My father is abdicating." She blurted it out without preamble. *So much for finesse.*

"What?"

"He wouldn't agree to end the engagement. I tried to reason with him, but he wouldn't back down. You met him. You saw what he's like."

"I did. He reminded me of my own father." Dalton rolled his eyes. "More than you know."

"Publishing my mother's diary was my only option. He knows once her words go public, the people of Delamotte will turn on him in a flash. He wants to step down before that can happen." Her father's pride came before anything. It had come before her mother. And in the end, it had been his downfall. He'd made the choice. Not her.

She'd done the only thing she could do. Letting go of the diary was her only option for getting her life back.

"Does this mean what I think it means?"

Aurélie nodded. "I'll be the Crown Princess. I'm going to rule Delamotte."

She took a deep inhale, did her best to ignore the hummingbird beat of her heart and said what she'd traveled 4,000 miles to tell him. "And I want you there with me. You and Jacques, of course."

Dalton Drake shot a glance at the dog and smiled the biggest smile she'd ever seen him display. "As luck would have it, I was already planning to visit your principality."

Is this truly happening? Is this real? "If you come...if you stay...it will mean leaving Drake Diamonds."

"Again, your timing is impeccable. I happen to be unemployed at the moment." He hauled her hard against him and brought his mouth down on hers in a powerful kiss that robbed her legs of strength.

Would she ever grow accustomed to this, she wondered. *Never.* There was magic in his touch. She was powerless against it. And she wouldn't have had it any other way.

She'd waited a lifetime for this kiss. She'd crisscrossed the globe and nearly toppled a kingdom.

It had been worth it. *He'd* been worth it.

"Excellent," she whispered against the wicked wonderland of his mouth. "Because I think you'd make a perfect Prince Consort."

"Are you asking me to marry you, Your Highness?" His eyes were shining. They seemed lighter than when she'd first met him. Soft pearl gray. "Right here in the Engagements showroom of Drake Diamonds?"

She nodded. "I am. And I just happen to know the cathedral is available three months from now."

He slid his hands down her arms, wove his fingers through hers and guided her gently backward, until she felt the cold press of a glass case against her bare back. He couldn't be serious. Half the city was downstairs. They didn't matter, though. No one did. Not now. Only them.

"No, princess." He reached behind her and slowly unzipped the bodice of her strapless gown. "Three months is far too long to wait to marry the woman I love. I want to make you my wife as soon as possible. Any chance we could get the cathedral sooner?"

Her dress slid down her body in a whisper of lilac, and she found herself naked once again in this glittering room, dressed in nothing but the cascade of gold pearls around her neck. "I think I can pull some strings."

"That's my princess."

My princess.

His princess.

His.

Dalton reached for her necklace, twirled the pearls slowly around his finger and used them to reel her in for a kiss. This time, the priceless string held tight, binding them together.

Forever unbroken.

* * * * *

Love awaits the Drake siblings in the glittering
world of jewels and New York City.

Don't miss Artem and Ophelia's tale
HIS BALLERINA BRIDE
and Diana's story in the final installment of
the DRAKE DIAMONDS trilogy
out July 2017 wherever Harlequin Special Edition
books and ebooks are sold.

www.Harlequin.com

Dear Reader,

This month—April 2017—marks the 35th anniversary for Harlequin Special Edition! Perhaps it's as hard for you, the reader, to believe this as it is for us, the team that has been presenting this warm, wonderful and relatable series of books for all these years. And while some of us are newer than others, the one thing that has always been consistent is that the Harlequin Special Edition lineup has always reached out and grabbed you, made you want to read more, made you look forward to what comes next.

April 2017 is a great illustration of this. We have *New York Times* bestselling author Brenda Novak in Harlequin Special Edition for the first time with *Finding Our Forever*, alongside our almost-brand-new author Katie Meyer with another in her Proposals in Paradise series, *The Groom's Little Girls*. We have *USA TODAY* bestselling and beloved authors Marie Ferrarella (*Meant to be Married*) and Judy Duarte in our next Fortunes of Texas: The Secret Fortunes story (*From Fortune to Family Man*). And if it's glamour, glitz and sparkle you want with your romance, look no further than *The Princess Problem* (next in the Drake Diamonds trilogy) by Teri Wilson.

We have moved through the last thirty-five years giving you, the reader, stories that warmed your heart and curled your toes, and we are just getting started! So happy anniversary...and here's to the next thirty-five!

Happy Reading,

Gail Chasan
Senior Editor, Harlequin Special Edition

Turn your love of reading into
rewards you'll love with
Harlequin My Rewards

**Join for FREE today at
www.HarlequinMyRewards.com**

Earn **FREE BOOKS** of your choice.

Experience **EXCLUSIVE OFFERS** and contests.

Enjoy **BOOK RECOMMENDATIONS**
selected just for you.

PLUS! Sign up now
and get **500** points
right away!

Earn
FREE
REWARDS
HarlequinMyRewards.com
Join
Today!

MYR16R

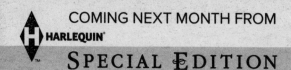
Available April 18, 2017

#2545 THE LAWMAN'S CONVENIENT BRIDE
The Bravos of Justice Creek • by Christine Rimmer
Jody Bravo has vowed to raise her baby alone and do it right. But Sheriff
Seth Yancy, whose deceased stepbrother is the father of Jody's child, is going
to protect and look after the baby and Jody—whether she wants his help or not.

#2546 CHARM SCHOOL FOR COWBOYS
Hurley's Homestyle Kitchen • by Meg Maxwell
When pregnant Emma Hurley starts a charm school for rancher Jake Morrow's
lovelorn cowboys, she never expected to enter into a fake engagement with
Jake. But when her father threatens to sell her family farm, Emma will do
whatever it takes to save it, even risk her heart!

#2547 HER KIND OF DOCTOR
Men of the West • by Stella Bagwell
Nurse Paige Winters and Dr. Luke Sherman have butted heads since they
started working in the ER together. But after she finally gives him a piece of
her mind and switches floors, Luke realizes Paige is much more than just
another nurse, and he's determined to prove he's exactly her kind of doctor!

#2548 FORTUNE'S SURPRISE ENGAGEMENT
The Fortunes of Texas: The Secret Fortunes
by Nancy Robards Thompson
Olivia Fortune Robinson has to prove to her sister that love is real, stat! So she
convinces everyone that she and Alejandro Mendoza are madly in love. And
when he proposes, she's just as shocked as everyone else. But his past loss
and her present cynicism threaten to keep this surprise engagement from
becoming the real thing.

#2549 THE LAST SINGLE GARRETT
Those Engaging Garretts! • by Brenda Harlen
When Josh Slater finds himself entrusted with the care of his three nieces
for the summer, he's forced to rely on his best friend's younger sister,
Tristyn Garrett, for help. But their attraction has simmered below the surface
for twelve years, and a summer spent on an RV road trip looks to be their
breaking point...

#2550 THE BRONC RIDER'S BABY
Rocking Chair Rodeo • by Judy Duarte
Former rodeo cowboy Nate Gallagher has just discovered he's the daddy of
a newborn baby girl—and starts falling for Anna Reynolds, the pretty social
worker assigned to assess whether he's true father material! Nate knows the
stakes are higher than ever. He's not just risking his heart, but a future for his
daughter.

**YOU CAN FIND MORE INFORMATION ON UPCOMING HARLEQUIN® TITLES,
FREE EXCERPTS AND MORE AT WWW.HARLEQUIN.COM.**

HSECNM0417

"Mirabelle's?" It was a new restaurant in town, a small, cozy place with white tablecloths and crystal chandeliers and a chef from New York. Everyone said the food was really good and the service impeccable.

"I heard it was good," he said. "Would you rather go somewhere else?"

"I just didn't know we were doing that."

"Doing what?"

"Going through with the date."

He set down his fork. "We're doing it." His voice was deep and rough, and his velvet-brown gaze caught hers and held it.

It just wasn't fair that the guy was so damn hot. *Not happening*, she reminded herself. *Don't get ideas.* "What about Marybeth?"

"It's only a few hours. Get a sitter. Maybe one of your sisters or maybe your mom."

"Ma? Please."

"She did raise five children, didn't she?"

"She's probably off on her next cruise already."

"A babysitter, Jody. I'm sure you can find one."

"But Marybeth is barely four weeks old."

"Jody. We're going. Stop making excuses."

She sagged back in her chair. "Why are you so determined about this?"

"Because I want to take you out."

"But…you don't go out, remember? There's no point because it can't go anywhere. Not to mention, I live in Broomtail County, and what if it got messy with me?"

"Too late." He was almost smiling. She could see that increasingly familiar twitch at the corner of his mouth. "It's already messy with you."

"I am not joking, Seth."

"Neither am I. I want to be with you, Jody. And not just as a friend."

"B-but I…" God. She was sputtering. And why did she suddenly feel light as a breath of air, as if she was floating on moonbeams? "You want to be with me? But you don't do that. You've made that very clear."

"You're right. I didn't do that. Until now. But things have changed."

"Because of Marybeth, you mean?"

"Yeah, because of Marybeth. And because of you, too. Because of the way you are. Strong and honest and smart and so pretty. Because we've got something going on, you and me. Something good. I'm through pretending that we're friends and nothing more. Are you telling me I'm the only one who feels that way?"

"I just…" Her pulse raced and her cheeks felt too hot. She'd promised herself that nothing like this would happen, that she wouldn't get her hopes up.

She needed to be careful. She could end up with her heart in pieces all over again.

Don't miss
THE LAWMAN'S CONVENIENT BRIDE
by Christine Rimmer, available May 2017 wherever
Harlequin® Special Edition books and ebooks are sold.

www.Harlequin.com

$1.⁰⁰ OFF

New York Times bestselling author
brenda novak

welcomes you to Silver Springs, a picturesque small town in Southern California where even the hardest hearts can learn to love again…

Available May 30, 2017.

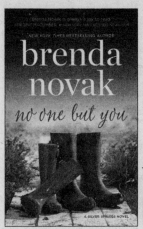

$7.99 U.S./$9.99 CAN.

$1.⁰⁰ OFF

the purchase price of NO ONE BUT YOU by Brenda Novak.

Offer valid from May 30, 2017, to June 30, 2017.
Redeemable at participating retail outlets, in-store only. Not redeemable at Barnes & Noble. Limit one coupon per purchase. Valid in the U.S.A. and Canada only.

52614662

5 65373 00076 2 (8100)0 12267

® and ™ are trademarks owned and used by the trademark owner and/or its licensee.

© 2017 Harlequin Enterprises Limited

MCOUPBN0617